Wooden Heart

DOCTOR·WHO

Wooden
Heart

MARTIN DAY

10 9 8 7 6 5 4 3

First published in 2007 by BBC Books, an imprint of Ebury Publishing.
A Random House Group Company.

This paperback edition published in 2013

Doctor Who is a BBC Wales production for BBC One
Executive Producers: Russell T Davies and Julie Gardner
Series Producer: Phil Collinson

The Random House Group Ltd Reg. No. 954009.

Addresses for companies within the Random House Group can be found at
www.randomhouse.co.uk.

A CIP catalogue record for this book is available from the British Library.

ISBN 9781849907651

Penguin Random House is committed to a sustainable future for
our business, our readers and our planet. This book is made from
Forest Stewardship Council® certified paper.

MIX
Paper from
responsible sources
FSC® C018179

Printed and bound in Great Britain by Clays Ltd, St Ives plc

Series Consultant: Justin Richards
Project Editor: Steve Tribe
Cover design by Henry Steadman © BBC 2007

Typeset in Albertina and Deviant Strain

Dedicated to the memory of
Craig Hinton

'He's gone,' said Petr in a choked whisper. 'Just like the others…'

Kristine pushed past her husband and into the room. She wanted to see for herself.

She stared at the crumpled sheets on the bed, the pale pillow that still bore an impression of her son's head. It looked for all the world as if Thom had simply got up to get a glass of water – as if he was in the next room and would soon return, rubbing his eyes and yawning.

Kristine rested a hand on the bed. It was warm.

'No,' she said at last. 'No, this can't be happening. Not to us…'

'Why should we be immune?' asked Petr. He tried to place a consoling arm around Kristine's waist, but she twisted free.

'The bars you put across the windows, the lock on the door…' There was anger in Kristine's voice now, an anger that her silent tears could not soften.

'We knew it might not make any difference,' said Petr. 'The children just disappear. There's no way of protecting them.'

Kristine shook her head. 'How can you be so accepting of it all?'

'I'm not,' said Petr, an awkward tone to his voice as he struggled with his emotions. 'But it's like I said. Just because Thom is the son of the elected leader, it does not make him any less vulnerable.'

'I don't care about the leadership,' said Kristine. 'I don't care about the village. I just want my son back!'

'I know,' said Petr.

This time Kristine accepted his embrace; he wrapped his arms around her, muffling the tears. Her entire body shook like a slender tree caught in the wind.

Petr shook his head sadly. 'If only this nightmare would end…'

'How many more children are going to disappear?' asked Kristine. 'How many more families are going to suffer?'

'I don't know,' said Petr. 'No one does.'

'We should ask for help.'

'But that is not our way,' said Petr, grateful that his wife was too weak to argue the point. 'This… evil… will either resolve itself or…'

'Or?'

'Or we must hope for outside intervention. Some

external factor, some *miracle* we have not considered – but you know we cannot make any approach ourselves.'

'So we do nothing?'

Petr didn't know what to say. In fact, he had tried every means at his disposal to protect the village from the gathering threat. But it was only now, after the evil had snatched away his own son, that he realised how pathetic their actions had been.

Just for a moment he thought he heard a footfall behind him – the creak of a floorboard, followed by the soft murmur of Thom's voice. But he knew his mind was playing tricks on him, and he wondered if Kristine was undergoing similar agonies.

'We're never going to see Thom again,' said Kristine in a voice so flat and hopeless it almost broke Petr's heart.

Petr thought of his son – such a proud, energetic child, forever tousle-haired and impish. Would he always be like that in Petr's mind, trapped in his youth and unable to grow older? Petr thought of Thom's strong hands, his clear eyes – his sheer force of will. And the arguments they'd had!

Petr would give anything in the world to have one last row with his son, just so that they could eventually come together to mumble their embarrassed apologies to each other. Just for one last chance to say how much he loved him.

'We'll see Thom again,' said Petr firmly. 'Somehow… Somehow all the children will come back to us.'

Kristine pulled away, a different dread in her eyes now. 'I know,' she said. 'That's what frightens me.'

ONE

For a few moments, as Martha stepped towards the main console, she thought she was alone.

The walls that pulsed with light, the huge support struts that seemed hewn from living coral, the mundane latticework beneath her feet – everything around her hummed with secrets and potential, with the hint of amazing things as yet unseen, and with terrifying things that were all too clear. It was like stepping into some old church where every footstep feels like an intrusion – or finding yourself alone in a mad scientist's lab and wondering which bubbling experiment or complex bit of machinery you'll fiddle with first.

She liked these moments without the Doctor – these momentary pauses for breath, when she had time to take it all in, to dwell on the things she had seen, the adventures she had already had. Paths already taken. Normal life never seemed so dull and one-dimensional as in these brief moments of reflection.

Then again, she didn't like having *too* much time to think – sometimes it was scary. These events that played out before her threatened, on occasion, to wash her away entirely. Sometimes she just wanted to watch a beautiful sunset on an alien world, or meet someone famous from history, without battalions of blood-sucking monsters and megalomaniacal villains hoving into view.

It was probably just as well, then, that at that moment she noticed the familiar and reassuring form of the Doctor, leaning against one of the walls, his face partly hidden by shadows, staring intently at the small scanner screen some feet away. He was chewing absent-mindedly on one of the arms of his glasses, seemingly lost in thought himself.

Martha circled around towards him and he looked up.

'It's just drifting through space,' he said, indicating the screen with his spectacles. 'It's easy to think that the cosmos is full of planets and stars and stuff, when actually… So much of it is empty. Bit of stray gas maybe, echoes of dark matter and plasma, but otherwise… Nothing.'

Martha came round and looked at the screen. It showed, as the Doctor said, a remarkably dark area of deep space. The velvety blackness was smudged by only a handful of distant stars. Against this there drifted the silent form of a slowly spinning craft. Orientated vertically, it resembled a great smooth tube of silver that thickened into some sort of blackened propulsion system at its base. At the top the tubular shape sprouted various spokes and protrusions.

'Every atom's full of space, isn't it?' she said. 'Even solid things… They're not really solid. Not if you look at them close enough.'

'The gap between electron and nucleus, the *chasm* between one atom and the next…'

'What's the ship?' asked Martha, looking back at the screen again.

'It's… interesting,' said the Doctor, as if that explained everything. 'A Century-class research vessel. The *Castor*, if the faint mayday signals it's giving off are to be believed. Not built for speed, as you can see – once it reached its destination it would hang around in orbit like a space station. Jack-of-all-trades sort of vessel.'

'What happened to it?'

'Dunno,' said the Doctor. 'No life signs, but no signs of collision or other damage either. I can't tell at the moment how long it's been here. Days, years, decades…' Suddenly his hands moved over the TARDIS controls in a blur. He spoke more quickly, a growing excitement evident in his voice. 'There's an atmosphere, though, and gravity – now that's odd in itself. And there's a few other little things as well…'

'Enough to pique your interest?'

'Oh yes!' he exclaimed, grinning. 'My interest is well and truly piqued. It's reached a critical level of piquedness. If it were any more piqued, I'd…' He slammed a few more controls home and very nearly pirouetted on the spot. 'I think I'd run out of pique and need a little lie-down!'

The great engines at the heart of the TARDIS began to wheeze and shudder.

'Are we going to take a look?' asked Martha, wondering if the Doctor could pick up the uncertainty in her voice. Exploring a rusting old space station stuffed with dead bodies – or worse – didn't exactly sound like a barrel of laughs. 'What am I saying?' she realised, seeing the Doctor's expression. 'Of course we're going to take a look.'

'So, why the *Castor*?' asked Martha some moments later as they stepped through the TARDIS doors and into darkness.

'Good question,' said the Doctor. He busied himself at a small panel on the wall, illuminated only by the piercing blue glow of his sonic screwdriver, then stepped backed triumphantly as the lights flickered on.

'*Fiat lux*!' he said triumphantly. 'From the Latin for *My small Italian car is on fire…*'

'They're not very bright,' said Martha. The lights that had come on were glowing dully, leaving pockets of shadow at regular intervals.

'Night cycle,' said the Doctor. He looked down the long, gently arcing corridor they found themselves in.

'I imagine whoever named this craft had a love of the classics.'

'Castor, as in Castor and Pollux – the sons of Leda,' said Martha, trying to elevate the conversation somewhat – and, if truth be told, wondering if she could impress the Doctor with her learning.

'That's right,' said the Doctor, peering at another panel recessed into the wall. 'Probably why on the colony world of Aractus they still say *Never turn your back on a swan.*'

Martha sighed. That was the problem with the Doctor – you had no way of working out if he was telling the truth, or deliberately escalating the conversation into the realms of the absurd. 'I'll remember that next time I'm on Aractus,' she said.

'Castor was said to be a skilled horse tamer,' said the Doctor, 'whereas Pollux was a pugnacious pugilist. I wonder if that has a bearing on this ship. People rarely just a pluck a name from the air – it always means something. Take Martha, for example…'

'Martha means "mistress of the house". I remember looking it up in the library when I was a kid.' Martha smiled. 'Mum just said she liked the sound of it.'

'There could be other reasons, I suppose,' said the Doctor. 'There's a place near Peterborough called Castor. Just off the A47…'

'So you're wondering if the owner of this spaceship was born near Peterborough…? Nothing against

Peterborough, but I prefer your first suggestion.'

'You do?' said the Doctor absent-mindedly as he pulled the mesh covering the panel clean off the wall. 'You should have heard my third idea…'

'Which was?'

'Whoever owned this ship was a fan of the Popeye cartoons.'

'Sorry?'

'Poor Popeye – hopelessly addicted to spinach and skinny women… Anyway, Olive Oyl's brother was called Castor.'

'You're a fount of useless information,' said Martha.

'Don't you mean "useful"?'

'I mean what I said.' She tried to see what the Doctor was doing. 'How come the lights are working?' she asked.

'Solar power,' said the Doctor, as if that explained everything.

'I've seen pictures of the space station,' said Martha. 'The one the Americans and the Soviets are building. They've got huge solar panels, but I didn't see anything like that on this ship.'

'It's integrated into the very fabric of the craft,' said the Doctor. 'Almost every external component and hull panel plays its part.'

'But you were just telling me how empty bits of space are. This thing might not have been anywhere near a sun for ages.'

The Doctor slipped on his glasses while peering at the panel's small read-out screen. 'It's obviously had just enough sunlight to keep it ticking over. To be fair, it hasn't had to expend much energy recently – a smidge on life support, a soupçon on a few other essential systems... The engines haven't been used in years, so it's just kind of drifted.'

'Is that what drew you here?' asked Martha. 'The mystery of it all – a *Mary Celeste* that drifts in the spaces between the stars...'

The Doctor took a step back, suddenly serious. 'It reminds me of another ship, a craft with a link to a person from the history of your planet...' He trailed away, his eyes intense, as if he could stare through the metal hull of the craft and see the stars and nebulae beyond.

'The *Pollux*?' suggested Martha hopefully.

'Never mind the *Pollux*,' said the Doctor abruptly, replacing what was left of the panel's outer covering. 'It's this vessel that fascinates me now. What happened here?'

He began to stride down the corridor; big, confident steps. Steps that wanted to march into the future, to turn corners, to find out what happened next – and to revel in it.

Martha chided herself for downplaying this particular trip in the TARDIS – she'd forgotten that, with the Doctor at your side, words like 'mundane' and 'everyday' just didn't seem to count.

'Probably just a systems malfunction,' offered Martha helpfully.

'There's no sign of any great systems failure in the central computer system,' said the Doctor. 'But perhaps it just healed itself. Stranger things have happened.'

Martha drew a long breath. 'If you say so.'

'Ah,' said the Doctor. 'This looks interesting.'

The corridor terminated at a circular door about three metres in diameter. It looked like a resolutely closed metal iris, and horizontal bars extended from the walls on either side and through large metal loops to give an even greater impression of solidity.

'To keep something out, or to lock something in?' wondered Martha out loud.

'My thoughts exactly,' said the Doctor. A quick wave of the sonic screwdriver and the bars retracted into the walls, leaving behind a faint smell of ozone and grease. Then the main door blossomed open.

'Hello!' the Doctor called as he stepped through. 'Anyone home?'

'You sure there's no one on board?' said Martha. 'Little bit of courtesy goes a long way, you know.'

'The TARDIS didn't pick up any life signs,' said the Doctor. 'As long as the life forms in question aren't hidden behind some sort of electromagnetic shield… Or out of phase…'

His voice dwindled to nothing as they found themselves on a high gantry, a circular walkway that had fifty or more doors leading away from it. Three metres above them was another walkway, and another; Martha risked a glimpse over the edge of the handrail, and the tubular structure they found themselves in seemed to disappear in both directions almost out of sight.

Martha took a step back from the edge. 'This place is *huge.*'

'It is,' agreed the Doctor. 'Any other thoughts?'

'It's very utilitarian,' said Martha.

The Doctor nodded. 'We know this is a research vessel and not a hotel, but even so… It's not at all what I was expecting.' He pointed to the identical doors, evenly spaced along this and all the other walkways. Each had a tiny observation window at head height. 'Remind you of anything?' he asked.

'A prison,' said Martha suddenly. 'It's like a huge prison.'

'I was worried you were going to say that,' said the Doctor, walking past Martha to the first door. He waved his sonic screwdriver over the control panel at the side of the cell. 'Shall we take a look?'

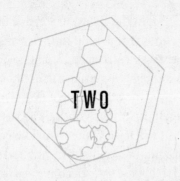

TWO

The door hummed open, a momentary interruption to the thick silence that gripped the vast chamber.

Martha paused, not sure what to expect. If you've encountered rhino-headed storm troopers and witches on broomsticks, she reasoned, you've got to keep your options open.

Nothing happened – nothing beyond a slight tingling sensation on her skin, as if the air in the cell, maintained for so long at a certain temperature and pressure, was now being released.

The Doctor stepped into the small room. 'It's perfectly safe,' he announced, though there was an ambiguity in his voice that did not inspire confidence.

When Martha followed him inside she understood the Doctor's uncertain tone.

The small area was no bigger than the box room at the front of the house where Martha had spent so much of her childhood. In the cell were a bed, a folding desk and a single cupboard high up in the corner of one of the walls. There was a screen at the far end of the room: whatever its original function, it resembled a dark, oversized tile as no power went to it now.

A few indeterminate items of clothing were scattered on the floor. A thick layer of dust had fallen on the desk and the pens and other items that cluttered its surface. 'No air filtration in here,' Martha observed in a whisper, remembering the pristine corridor they had landed in.

'No,' said the Doctor, his own voice a funereal whisper. 'Not a high enough priority, I suppose.'

Martha reached out to run her finger across the desk, then remembered that household dust was largely composed of shed human skin. She shivered, staring intently at the object of the Doctor's curiosity, for lying in the bunk, curled as if sleeping, was the long-dead body of a man, tatters of bleached-grey overall still clinging to his limbs.

'How long has he been dead?' she asked, appalled but unable to avert her gaze from the cracked, shrivelled skin.

The Doctor popped his glasses back on his nose, dropping his head to look more closely at the dead man than even Martha, with all her medical training to back her up, would have been comfortable with. 'What with the somewhat garbled information I was able to glean from the central computer, and given the obvious age of his body...' He paused. 'Whatever happened on this craft, it all took place at least a hundred years ago.'

'A hundred years?'

'Yeah, give or take. The artificial atmosphere means the corpse has become… sort of mummified. The outer few layers of the epidermis have gone' – Martha glanced at the dust again and a shiver went down her spine – 'but the rest of the body has just… dried out.'

The Doctor turned to look at Martha, his body language reassuring despite his words and the environment they found themselves in.

'So sad,' he added, quietly.

'Any idea what killed him?' Martha asked, opening up the cupboard but finding only two small porcelain figures and a thick paperback book.

'Dunno,' said the Doctor, slipping his glasses into a pocket. 'How do you fancy putting your training in pathology to the test?'

'Not absolutely number one on my list of things to do in the next five minutes,' said Martha.

'So perhaps we'd better find another way. Less… invasive.' He turned for the door. 'What was the book in the cupboard, by the way?'

'Freud's *Interpretations of Dreams*,' said Martha, pleased to be following him out of the room.

The Doctor nodded, then pointed to the control panel set into the doorway. 'You can only open the cell doors from outside,' he said. 'This part of the ship… It's definitely a prison.'

'What would a prison be doing on a research vessel?' asked Martha.

'Depends what it's researching.' His voice became deadly serious. 'But I think we just found our first guinea pig.'

They stood for a moment on the circular gantry, Martha marvelling at the sheer size of the place. On the TARDIS scanners it was hard to get a sense of scale just by looking at something against the backdrop of space. As a result she'd been expecting something grim and claustrophobic, like the Russian-American space station she had mentioned to the Doctor. The reality, however, was a vast expanse of endless alloy and open space.

Mind you, the cell had been grim and claustrophobic – the prisoners here, if that's what they were, certainly hadn't been living the life of Riley.

She turned to the Doctor, still thinking of the few items she'd found in the cupboard. 'I'm surprised that people in the future still have books,' she said. 'The way technology advances, I thought you'd… Plug yourself into a computer and download stuff straight into your brain.'

'Even when something new and flashy comes along,' observed the Doctor, 'the old forms persist. You should see my record collection! Can't beat a good bit of vinyl.'

He started to make his way to the next cell along.

'Anyway,' he continued, 'what could be more practical than a real, old book made from real, old bits of paper?

You can read it in bed, on a bus, in the bath even. You try doing that with a PDA when the batteries are flat!' He held the sonic screwdriver over the door, glancing at Martha. 'Ready?'

She nodded, and he waved his hand over the keypad like a magician with a wand. A glow of light, a briefly oscillating noise as the screwdriver doubtless tried every possible combination under the sun, and then the door hissed open.

The room beyond was almost identical to the first. The final pose of the body it contained couldn't have been more different, however. If the first prisoner they had stumbled across had perhaps died in his sleep, this one had pushed himself into the corner of the room and pulled his knees up to his chest. Though slumped now, Martha could imagine the arms being coiled tightly over his ears and eyes, trying to block out… What?

She shivered. 'Any signs of trauma?' she asked.

The Doctor leant forward. 'No… Nothing obvious.'

'The life support must have failed.'

'But the computer says life support's been ticking over with barely a problem since it first came into service.'

They tried the next cell, and the next, and the next. Each contained a body, shrivelled by the unique atmospherics of the craft. It was not obvious why any of them had died. The Doctor and Martha checked a few more, finding yet more corpses, some apparently sleeping, some apparently frozen as if in flight from an unseen terror. None, of course, could escape, for each cell had remained resolutely locked. As the Doctor observed, the entire place seemed ruthlessly efficient – it was a testament to human ingenuity that it was all still working after so long.

'I don't think we're going to find anything more here,' said the Doctor.

Martha was relieved – she didn't much fancy spending the rest of the day checking the other cells. There were hundreds of them, and there was no reason to expect that any of them would be any different from those they had already examined.

'We need to find the technical area,' said the Doctor. 'There's a limit to what the computer systems I can hack into from here can tell me.'

Martha risked a glance over her shoulder as she walked. 'All these prisoners… Were they criminals or political activists or captured soldiers or…?'

'Yeah, that's one of the questions I'm keen to answer,' said the Doctor. 'If we can—'

He stopped suddenly, Martha almost running into the back of him.

'Did you hear that?' he whispered, his head darting from side to side.

'What?' Martha hissed, suddenly more on edge. The only thing worse than exploring a mausoleum full of bodies was the idea that someone or something in there wasn't quite dead yet.

'I thought I heard something,' said the Doctor. He paused for a moment, then carried on walking, head held high, as if nothing was the matter. 'Oh, well, not to worry,' he said loudly.

'Not to worry?'

'This place has been shut up for a hundred years,' he continued. 'No movements, no disturbances – and then we come along, breathing in the air, opening doors, generally making a nuisance of ourselves…'

'Speak for yourself,' said Martha.

'Plenty of creaks and groans, but absolutely nothing to worry about!' He grinned brightly, and just for a moment Martha was taken in by his broad smile – the sort of innocent grin that, on Earth, usually went with scraped knees and *Sorry, miss, my mate's just hoofed our football over your garden wall, you don't mind if we go and get it, do you…?*

Then she noticed that she couldn't see one of the Doctor's hands.

'You've got your fingers crossed behind your back, haven't you?'

The Doctor was immediately on the defensive. 'Who, me? Fingers crossed? Nah, never!'

Only moments later did his left hand emerge to start inputting the correct settings on the sonic screwdriver.

Beyond the second irised door the Doctor and Martha found a much more high-tech series of corridors and rooms. The night-time lighting illuminated myriad machines and a bewildering array of desks, workstations and control panels.

'This is more like it!' exclaimed the Doctor.

They found yet more corpses, just as hideous as those they'd previously encountered, but some wore security uniforms, while others were in long white coats. 'Scientists?' speculated Martha. 'You said they were researching something here.'

'And hired muscle,' said the Doctor, bending over the body of one particular guard, frozen in position over a bank of computer screens. A quick glance and you could almost imagine he was still doing his job, still watching the security camera images for the slightest signs of trouble. The monitors, though, had long since powered off.

The Doctor waved his hands over what appeared to be some sort of keyboard made of thick fibre optic strands. 'One thing you can say about the people of your future, Martha… Is that they've long since abandoned screensavers… This monitor will go into complete hibernation if it doesn't detect any movement – and I'm talking blinking eyes, scratching your head, that sort of thing. Very green, *and* it stops the guards from falling asleep on the job.'

'But that's exactly what seems to have happened, isn't it?' said Martha. 'It's like everyone just fell asleep.'

'Hmm…' The Doctor didn't sound convinced.

The screen, as if it resented the intrusion after all these years of slumber, finally sprang into life. Martha noticed that others stretched along the long panel in front of them were also beginning to glow. Every one showed a section of the multi-level prison area they had just been in; the view cycled from one hidden camera to another, and it was only the subtleties of light and shade that made each snapshot different from the last. Being a guard on this ship, reflected Martha, must have been dull in the extreme.

Before the Doctor could say anything, the lights in the room – mere glowing pinpricks against the flat, dull ceiling – became gradually brighter. The room moved from a subtle sense of autumnal night to the artificial cold-blue harshness of a working day. A quick glance at the images on the monitors, and into the corridor behind them, revealed the truth. It was as if the Doctor and Martha had intruded into some magical, slumbering kingdom, which all around them was beginning to wake.

'What have you done?' Martha blurted out, surprised at her own reaction. She would have expected to have welcomed the light and brightness, but, surrounded as she was by hundred-year-old corpses, everything seemed even more grotesque now. It just seemed wrong somehow, like stumbling into a funeral with hats and party poppers.

'The daylight cycle's kicked in,' said the Doctor. 'Nothing to do with me. Honest.'

Even so, Martha found herself glancing over her shoulder to make sure that they were still alone.

'Now we're cooking with gas!' exclaimed the Doctor, settling down at an unoccupied console, his hands blurring over the controls. Martha watched him for a moment, but he seemed now only to be conversing with himself, muttering occasionally and sighing.

Martha turned away, feeling both lost and useless in this futuristic environment. 'This is the point,' the Doctor suddenly whispered, without looking up, 'where curiosity usually gets the better of people. It has been known for my friends to go for a wander, get lost, or stumble upon something quite unexpected...'

'Go for a walk around here?' scoffed Martha. 'Are you serious?' She strolled over to another console – at least this room seemed safe enough. 'You know, I think I'll take you to Kensal Green cemetery if we ever get back to London,' she said, warming to her theme. 'Consider it... repayment in kind.'

'Oh, I love cemeteries!' exclaimed the Doctor happily.

'You would,' muttered Martha, just quietly enough for the Doctor not to hear.

'Isn't Brunel buried there? And Thackeray – I told him to paint those pillar boxes red, you know. He really wanted them in yellow! And Oscar Wilde's dear old mum.'

'Doctor...'

'Oh, and Charles Blondin, of course! Do you know, when he took me across the Niagara Falls in that wheelbarrow, well, for once, I feared for my life…'

'Doctor!'

'Hmm?' the Doctor looked up from his screen.

'There's something you should see,' said Martha, wondering if he could detect the fear in her voice.

Within a moment he was at her side. 'What is it?'

Martha pointed at the display in front of her. Something had caught her eye – and it made her blood run cold. 'I thought you said there were no life signs on this ship.'

'No, there weren't – though, if you remember, I did add certain caveats, a few qualifications…'

'Well,' said Martha, tapping the screen for emphasis, 'we're certainly not on our own any more.'

'Ah,' said the Doctor slowly. He stared at the monitor, turned his head away, and then looked back at the information – as if checking he wasn't mistaken. The readings were still there.

'Ah,' said the Doctor again.

'Ah?'

'Definitely,' he said. He glanced at Martha. 'Doesn't make sense, does it?'

'Phew,' said Martha. 'I thought it was just me.'

The monitor showed a map of the *Castor*, each level, room and wing picked out in fine detail. Coloured dots marked the presence of life on the ship. 'There's us,' said the Doctor, indicating two strands of information scrolling across the screen. 'One human, one *unknown* – how rude! It says we're both standing in Security Room B, that we're both physically fit, and… Oh, bad luck, Martha!'

'What?'

'Says you're developing an ear infection. Something to watch out for. Or listen out for maybe.'

'Honestly, I feel fine,' said Martha.

'Computer says *No*,' said the Doctor. 'And we can't argue with this fine piece of hardware, can we? Not when it has just detected these other signs of life…'

He stabbed at two other dots with strips of information scrolling off them. One strand seemed awash with information, and one barely seemed to register at all. Indeed, as she peered still more closely, the fourth data stream blinked out completely.

'Look!' she said. 'It's gone.'

'And then there were three,' said the Doctor gravely. 'Well, I say three, but this other life sign… It's like trying to isolate a footballer's broken leg by taking an X-ray of the entire team. Just too much data, all in one go! The system is struggling to isolate any meaningful information.'

'And the one that's just disappeared?'

'The exact opposite – no real data worth gathering. No heat, no energy, no movement… Oh, look, it's come back again!'

The fourth dot appeared again, flickering like a torch running on old batteries.

'You reckon you can work out where on the ship these… life forms are?' asked Martha.

'Absolutely! That big *splurge* of info shouldn't be too hard to keep an eye on. Not so sure about the other fella, though – more like a shadow than a real creature at all.' His voice became a whisper. 'Between the idea and the reality… Falls the shadow.'

'Then let's find out where the big one's coming from,' said Martha.

The Doctor pressed a few buttons, whistling under his breath. 'Just look at the energy that creature's pumping out!' he exclaimed moments later. 'Hook him, her or it up to the national grid and you could power Milton Keynes for a week!'

'Why Milton Keynes?'

'Why *not* Milton Keynes?' said the Doctor. 'You know, whenever a chunk of the Amazon rainforest disappears, it's always a piece of land the size of Wales. Or Belgium. What have they ever done to anyone?' He found a pen in an inside pocket and scribbled some coordinates on the back of his hand. 'Bad news,' he said as he did so.

'What is?'

'This big life sign the computer's picked up…' He sighed. 'It's between us and the TARDIS.'

The Doctor and Martha left the security room only

after checking all the available monitors. There didn't seem to be any cameras trained on the spot the Doctor had identified – the fourth reading having faded away to nothing once more – but everywhere else seemed as bland and empty as before. The cells were, as they had left them, all securely locked; the corridors and other chambers were bereft of life and movement.

They headed back the way they had come, past the dead guards and the rooms filled with slumbering equipment. It was horrible, Martha considered, but, with one identical corridor after another, she was starting to navigate by the bodies they passed. Just opposite Security Room B was a cadaver in a pale, tattered coat; it was conceivable that this person had been running from some assailant or threat. Left turn at the remains of a guard, slumped against a wall as if exhausted, then right at a corpse perched atop a metal stool with its skeletal hand still resting on the keyboard in front of it.

After a few moments they found themselves at the rounded hatch; it spiralled open and they stepped onto the walkway that encircled the prison area. Their footsteps seemed quieter and less obtrusive now that all the lights were blazing, but, even so, Martha kept glancing over her shoulder. At one point she was convinced she heard something clang somewhere, like a door slamming shut or something heavy and resonant hitting a floor. She glanced at the Doctor, who behaved as if he had heard nothing, striding powerfully towards his beloved TARDIS. In fact, he hadn't really spoken since they'd left the room with the security monitors.

'So,' Martha ventured, 'any ideas yet what happened to these poor people?'

'Oh, I have one or two thoughts,' said the Doctor with an attempt at breezy indifference, though he lapsed into silence immediately.

Martha waited, but nothing else was forthcoming. 'Such as?' she said eventually.

'Oh…' The Doctor sighed, slowing a little. 'Something almost instantaneous – minutes rather than hours. And something that didn't involve the ship itself – all the systems do seem to be working perfectly.'

'So it must have been something like… a quick-acting virus.'

'That would be one way of putting it,' agreed the Doctor.

There was another long pause. Martha knew they must be nearing the TARDIS by now. 'What I don't understand,' she said, 'is why no one came to reclaim the ship. I know human life can be cheap, but surely this vessel itself must be worth a few quid to someone. And the families of the deceased must have been pestering the authorities to get the bodies back…'

'Perhaps they tried,' said the Doctor. 'They tried, and failed, and so resigned this place to its fate. So they left it to float into eternity – a ghost ship on an endless voyage.'

'You don't think we're infected, do you?' asked Martha, suddenly panicked. 'If the authorities put this place under quarantine…'

'Don't worry,' said the Doctor. 'The scanners would have picked something up – like they did with your ear!'

'There's nothing wrong with my ear!' said Martha, though, now she thought about it, she did feel a slight pressure on one side of her face.

'Anyway,' said the Doctor. 'I don't think it was an illness as such.'

'What then?' Martha paused. 'This creature?'

'Possibly. The life signs were puzzling in the extreme.'

'And we're just going to wander up and say, "Hi, why did you kill all the people on this ship, and, by the way, do you mind if we just squeeze past you and get back to the TARDIS?"'

'That's about the size of it, yeah,' said the Doctor.

They turned a corner and came to a halt at a rough metal door.

'It should be just the other side,' he said.

'I don't remember this door being here before,' said Martha.

'I'm not sure it was. Perhaps it's only used during the day.'

'Or perhaps something triggered it,' said Martha, grimly.

The Doctor said nothing, but held up his sonic screwdriver. 'Shall we?'

'Go on then.'

The screwdriver flashed for a moment, and then the door slid open.

There was a long pause before either of them spoke. 'Now I might be mistaken,' said the Doctor, 'but we didn't leave the TARDIS parked in a forest, did we?'

THREE

The sun rose into the ocean-blue sky, a burning disk that ignited thin streamers of cloud on the horizon. The light picked out the edges of distant purple mountains, the ripples in the great grey lake, the tips of the angular trees as they shook in the early morning breeze. The entire forest, at night a shapeless and still slab of interlocking darkness and shadow, began to stir. A deer appeared between the trees and looked around nervously before making its way to the lake's edge to drink.

The burning ribbons of cloud appeared to reach out towards the village, where they merged with the elongated garlands of scarlet that fluttered from the flagpoles and the arched bridges.

Breathing deeply, Saul gripped the rough wooden handrail, as if the sheer beauty of the scene would overwhelm him. The splashing, impossibly clear waters that cascaded beneath the bridge seemed unfathomable, unanswerable, yet they pointed to something beyond Saul's everyday life. He knew neither the river's source, nor its eventual outflow into some larger body of water – for some people, merely having the river running beneath their feet would be enough. They would savour the moment, or use it as part of the fabric to dress their mundane lives. But Saul wanted more.

Saul always wanted more.

Everyday life did eventually disturb Saul's thoughts, though he did not resent the intrusion. He was usually the first to rise, but this morning he'd only had a few minutes to himself before he'd heard the rattle of shutters and the creak of doors. He glanced over at the square at the heart of the village and could see children playing in the dewy grass before breakfast; elsewhere adults were emerging to feed animals or check the fields.

Saul smiled. Just for a moment it was possible to imagine that everything was all right, that the day would be uninterrupted by grief and loss. However, as Saul turned on the bridge to head back home, he glimpsed again the lake to the north. The water was the colour of slate, and mist was just beginning to form at its edge, obscuring the tiny, mysterious island at the lake's centre. The fog, thick and knotted like old rope, began to expand even as Saul watched it. This wasn't fog that the rising sun could burn away.

This wasn't normal fog at all.

Saul turned his back on the lake and the island, making his way down to a stony area at the side of the river. He was carrying a painted ceramic pitcher on his back, looped around his shoulders with long strips of black leather, and he spent a few moments dropping this down and into the clear water. It wasn't much, but then the old woman needed little to get her through the day. It would suffice.

Pushing the wooden stopper into place, he hefted the pitcher onto his back, and set off for the woman's house. It was at the edge of the village, its sloping roof only just catching the light of the sun. The Dazai's house was angled away from most of its neighbours, its doorway opening not onto the village but onto the forest. It made sure that every visitor actually intended to see her; no one passed by on their way somewhere else.

Saul knocked on the door, setting the pitcher down on its flattened base. When the Dazai slid back the door, he bowed low. 'Good morning,' he said simply.

The Dazai bowed in return. 'My blessings to you, child.' Her voice crackled like dead leaves and dry wood. 'You have brought my water?'

'As always, noble Dazai.'

'I am honoured. You are like a son to me, Saul. Would you like to come in?'

Every morning, without fail, the Dazai made the same offer. He only ever accepted when there was something on his mind. 'If I may…?'

'Of course.' Despite being bent double with age, the Dazai picked up the water pitcher effortlessly and shuffled inside. Saul followed the old woman into a perfectly square room with a large bookcase dominating one wall. A wooden table and four chairs sat at its centre, though it was well known in the village that the Dazai rarely saw more than a single person at a time. One person was an audience, a consultation; more than that was a party, and the Dazai was too old to approve of *them*.

'How is your brother?' she asked, gesturing that Saul should sit.

'Busy,' said Saul. The dismissive word sounded more bitter than he had intended. 'I do not envy Petr his position,' he added hastily. 'He has a lot on his mind.'

'We all have a lot on our minds,' observed the Dazai, 'and only a fool would envy a diligent leader his position in life. Better by far to be indolent or carefree or selfish.'

'I'm often accused of being all those things…'

'Then they do not know you as well as I do. I know you care – and care deeply. To be lazy or self-serving – it's the easy way.' She raised a finger, as brown and knotted as a twig from the forest floor. 'I am not, of course, saying it is the *best* way.' She poured Saul some tea from a large copper kettle. 'You and Petr are more alike than either of you care to admit.'

'Perhaps,' said Saul. He took the tiny tumbler of tea, tipping it first one way, then another. Were it not for the steam rising from it, the tea would appear as cold and grey as the great lake that lapped against the edges of the village.

He drained the tumbler in one, and slid it back across the table.

'What do you think this day will bring, noble Dazai?' The Dazai continued to stare at Saul and he found himself unable to hold her gaze. 'The fog's already gathering,' he added.

'I feel it will bring something new,' said the Dazai. 'Whether for good or ill…' She paused, as if sniffing the air for clues. 'No, I cannot tell.' She indicated the kettle. 'Another?'

Saul got to his feet, bowing again. 'I need to check my traps in the forest,' he said. 'And then I need to speak to my brother.'

'You still wish to travel to the outer settlements?'

'I need to see what's there,' said Saul. 'Perhaps they can help us… With the children, I mean.'

The Dazai shook her head. 'The children are beyond our help now,' she said gravely. 'Let us hope that *we* do not join them.'

Martha took another deep breath. 'I don't believe it…' she said slowly.

'So you've said.' The Doctor, his hands deep in his pockets, looked around once more, like a child desperately trying to work out how a conjuring trick is done. 'Twice,' he added.

'But – we were on a spaceship. We opened a door…'

'And wallop!' said the Doctor. 'Here we are.'

Martha and the Doctor stood in a small clearing in a forest, surrounded by thin autumnal trees and angular evergreens. There was a thick carpet of bronze-coloured leaves under their feet, and over their heads the circle of blue sky was unblemished but for a pale curl of cloud.

'*That* should be deep space,' said Martha, pointing upwards. 'You know, black, full of stars… And this…' She bent down, forcing her hands through the leaves. 'This should be a metal floor. The TARDIS should be just in front of us!'

'Perhaps it is,' said the Doctor. 'And we just can't see it.'

'So this is some sort of… virtual reality? A computer simulation or something?'

'I don't think so,' said the Doctor, cautiously.

Martha picked up a leaf by its stalk, twirled it between her fingers, held it up to the sunlight. It was large, copper-coloured and webbed by deep green veins, as angular as a child's drawing of a splayed hand. 'It all feels pretty real,' she said.

And there were the sounds, too – tiny sounds of furtive animals foraging through the undergrowth, joyful birdsong high up in the trees. More distantly, an intermittent thrumming of a woodpecker tapping against rotten wood.

'It smells pretty real, too,' said the Doctor, who for his part had found a fungus at the root of a tree. He passed it to Martha – a white streak of flesh peppered with vivid red spots, like a comedy toadstool.

Martha breathed deeply – and immediately wished she hadn't. 'It stinks!' she said.

'Student's sock with a hint of back-of-fridge Cheddar,' grinned the Doctor.

'We've gone through… some sort of portal, then,' said Martha, desperate to make sense of their situation. 'We walked through, and… Now we're on another world.'

'I don't remember stepping through a magic wardrobe, do you?'

Martha was getting impatient with the Doctor's wilful misreading of her comments. 'No, you know… A wormhole that links one bit of space and time with another.'

'You ever seen a wormhole?' queried the Doctor.

'You know I haven't!'

'Well, it's nothing like this. Anyway, take a look there.' He pointed over Martha's shoulder.

Behind her, as if drawn on the gnarled trunk in spots of pale lichen, was the faintest impression of the door they had just walked through – a rounded, metallic, very real door. Part of a very real space station that, in the blink of an eye, had been replaced by a clearing in the forest.

Martha rapped the back of her hand against the tree.

It made a metallic clang, as if the entire tree were made of steel.

'So this clearing, this forest… It's *attached* to the *Castor*?'

'It seems to be, doesn't it?' The Doctor was on his hands and knees again, digging down through the layer of leaves near the metallic tree. He eventually found a small section of the space station floor, glinting in the light of an impossible sun.

Martha tapped her foot on the revealed metal floor. 'Can we get back?'

'To the station? Don't know. Haven't tried yet.' He walked off. 'Aren't you intrigued, though? Don't you want to see if this forest goes anywhere, or if it just turns into another chunk of spaceship?'

Martha considered. She supposed the forest was preferable to a space station full of dust and bodies. And there was always the chance that they'd find themselves back in the research craft before too long – or maybe even back in the TARDIS. 'It is beautiful,' she admitted. 'OK, just a quick look.'

'Of course,' said the Doctor.

'On the understanding that we're really only looking for the TARDIS.'

'Absolutely.'

'And that we can find our way back to this point without a problem.'

'Piece of cake,' said the Doctor.

'And that we'll be gone for no more than five minutes.'

'Five minutes. Max.'

Two hours later and they were still going. Martha wasn't convinced that this was because they were in an especially large forest; instead, she suspected that they were simply going round in circles. Every few minutes they would pass a tree stump that looked like the head of a bloated teddy bear. She tried pointing this out to the Doctor, but he seemed as sanguine as ever. He mentioned something about going astray with the Brothers Grimm, commented airily on why lost people so often walk in circles – something to do with the inner ear, if Martha recalled correctly – and then asked her how she was feeling.

Martha's gloom deepened. The medical scanner on the research ship had been right after all – her ear *was* starting to hurt. When she put a finger to it, it felt hot and inflamed. The sooner they got back to the relative comfort of the TARDIS, the better.

'Not far to go now,' said the Doctor cheerfully.

'What do you mean? We've been wandering around for ages!'

'I mean, just a few more minutes and then we'll go back.'

'Are you sure we *can* go back?' asked Martha.

'Just a few more minutes,' said the Doctor, ducking the question.

As they walked, the Doctor would gesture towards a brightly coloured flower in a glade or a brightly trilling yellow bird in the uppermost branches. At one point, they heard something crashing through the undergrowth, and they both paused, nervously eyeing each other and the gently swaying trees that, just for a moment, appeared to lean towards them.

Then, a tiny boar, dappled with yellow and brown stripes, hurtled out of the trees, squealing. It appeared to glance up at the Doctor and Martha as it moved and then, shrieking all the louder, turned and crashed back into the forest.

Quick as a flash the Doctor pulled his sonic screwdriver from a pocket and shone it at the retreating creature. 'Interesting,' he said, thoughtfully.

'It is?' said Martha.

'Yeah,' said the Doctor. 'Not quite alive. Well, not in the same way that you and I are.' And he turned the brilliant blue light onto Martha.

'Oi!' said Martha. 'Cut it out!'

The Doctor grinned, putting the screwdriver away before setting off. Martha hurried to catch up.

'So, what was that creature?' asked Martha.

'It appeared to be a wild boar,' said the Doctor. '*Sus scrofa* – still common in central Europe, even in your time. Then again,' he went on, 'I've seen pagoda trees from Asia, magnolias unique to North America… Frankly, half of the trees in this forest don't belong together, and

I'm not sure I even recognise the other half.'

'Not from Earth?'

'Not from any planet I know,' said the Doctor. 'And I always got top marks for botany at school!'

Martha pointed back in the direction they'd come. 'Let's turn round. There's no sign of the TARDIS, no sign of the forest's edge. Maybe we can work out what's going on from the space station.'

The Doctor stopped suddenly. 'Excellent idea,' he said.

Martha, sighing, circled on the spot and started to walk away. Then she noticed the Doctor wasn't coming and she looked back at him.

'One slight problem,' the Doctor continued, still rooted to the spot.

'Yeah?'

'I'm caught in a trap,' said the Doctor, pointing down to something metallic at his feet. For the first time Martha could see the beads of sweat on the Doctor's forehead. 'Doesn't half hurt,' he added.

FOUR

Saul moved through the forest silently, but at speed. Something was wrong. The equilibrium of the forest had been disturbed, possibly by some rogue element – a new predator, perhaps? He wasn't unduly surprised. With all that was going on in the village, it was surely only a matter of time before the unease and disruption spread further afield.

He'd found nothing in his rope traps, though the bait had gone from a couple. The wolves – or whatever they were – seemed to be getting cleverer by the day. Still, it only took one slip, one newcomer to the forest who didn't recognise the tell-tale signs… Saul had replaced the meat before heading off to the traps in the north and west of the forest. He hoped he'd have better luck there.

As he approached the area, his sense of unease deepened. His shoulders prickled and his mouth became dry.

He could hear voices.

'I can't really get a good grip on it.' A woman's voice.

'Ow, that hurts!' A man – in some discomfort.

'Look, I'm trying my best!'

Saul was about to march into the clearing – this was Saul's area, surely they knew better than to come up here? – when he realised that he recognised neither voice. They spoke in clipped, rushed words, and that wasn't just a result of the trap. These were people used to living life at speed, and the pain in the man's voice was as much irritation at an interruption as a genuine fear for his own life.

Saul paused for a moment, his hand on the short sword that he always carried at his side. Who were these people? Traders did, on occasion, come to the village – almost always seeming to trigger yet another argument between Saul and his brother – but invariably word was sent ahead of them. Saul was sure that no emissaries or merchants were expected, and even if they were lone individuals seeking some sort of business opportunity, why would they try to approach the village from the woods? Much easier to take a route down from the mountains.

Perhaps, then, these individuals had a more malign agenda – perhaps it was their presence that had so disrupted the forest. Perhaps, even, they were responsible for the succession of recent, grim events, though, as he crept forward, Saul had to admit to himself that they didn't sound terribly sinister.

Incompetent, perhaps, but not sinister.

'Now I've got my finger stuck!'

'Doctor, you're not helping. Look, let's wipe away the worst of the blood and try to get a good look…'

Saul settled behind a squat flowering shrub and gently parted the leaves. There were two outsiders, completely unknown to him. The man was dressed in a subdued manner, as if he wished to wear nothing that would detract from the expressive force of his own personality. The woman, on the other hand, was as brightly coloured as a flower desperate for the attention of a life-giving bee. Her clothing was a kaleidoscope of hues and textures and her dark hair resembled the crest of some exotic songbird.

The more he considered it, the more Saul concluded that – whoever they were – these people were not a threat. And, if that was true, then what – or who – had caused such a palpable shift in the atmosphere in the woods?

Pushing these concerns to the back of his mind, Saul was about to rise from his position and greet the outsiders when he heard a twig crack, far away to his right.

The woods – despite the constant, frantic bickering of the couple in the clearing – became quieter still. Saul, holding his breath, moved his head slowly in the direction of the sound.

He could sense that something was coming, alerted by the sounds of the trapped man and his friend. Something grim and purposeful, something as different from bear or wolf as he himself was from a hen or a swan.

Something huge and threatening, something from legend, was advancing towards them.

Petr found the Dazai sitting on the steps that led up to her home, regarding the trees of the forest's edge as intently as one would pore over an ancient document. Her broad forehead had cracked into a puzzled frown, but something like a smile played out on the edges of her lips.

Petr stood for a few moments, unsure if the Dazai had heard him coming. 'Noble Dazai,' he began after a few moments – as irritated as ever by the lack of authority and assurance in his voice.

'I heard you,' snapped the Dazai, still regarding the dark, swaying trees. 'Unlike your brother, you thunder around with all the subtlety of an amorous bull!'

'Noble Dazai,' said Petr, swallowing down his embarrassment, 'I did not mean to…'

'Shh!' she hissed, a finger appearing at her lips. 'Something is going on, deep in the trees…' She paused, her eyes active – and then sighed, turning to Petr. 'Ah, the moment has gone,' she complained. 'We will find out soon enough.'

'I am sorry,' said Petr, bowing low.

'What do you want?' snapped the Dazai, her eyes still blazing. Then, as Petr stood there, trying to clear his throat and formulate what he wanted to say, she seemed to cast off her irritation like a discarded cloak. She rose, unsteadily, to her feet and, one hand gripping a cane tightly, extended the other to lightly touch Petr's arm. 'Come, you can tell me as we stroll through the village. A walk will do me good.'

Without asking, the Dazai looped her arm through Petr's. They began to head towards the village green and Petr's formal hall at its far side.

'My brother came here this morning,' Petr said simply. He knew it was better to be blunt with the Dazai; she disliked many things, and needless embellishment was one of them.

'Who told you?' she asked, though her former irritability had subsided. It was a question, not a criticism.

'I saw him myself,' said Petr. 'I did not sleep well, and was watching over the village before sunrise.'

'Hoping that your own attentiveness might save the children?'

'Or prevent them from returning to us, yes,' said Petr. 'If I could, by my own actions, save our village from its fate…'

The Dazai glanced at Petr. Her voice became quieter still. 'Noble Petr… You would indeed do anything to save your subjects.'

'They are my family,' said Petr simply.

'Indeed they are,' said the Dazai. 'Why do you ask about your birth brother? It is no secret that he fetches me water each morning.'

'Forgive me, noble Dazai, but… I need to know if the two of you have discussed anything regarding this… situation.'

'Your brother is a loyal subject,' said the Dazai. 'Though his roving spirit would love to travel the land far and wide, he accepts the judgement that you have handed down and contents himself within the forest. In all the time we have spoken he has never once expressed resentment or frustration.' The Dazai paused for a moment, her eyes full of affection. 'He would do nothing to undermine you or to risk the good of this village. If he had some insight or knowledge, he would bring it to you. You must know that.'

'I know that he was your favourite to become leader.'

The Dazai continued on her way, leaning even more heavily now against Petr's side. 'That is true. Your brother has many noble qualities – a man of action, a man impatient for change and progress, a man with drive.' The Dazai chuckled. 'But the village council wanted a thinker, a deliberator, a man more used to weighing up matters than coming to an impulsive conclusion. And, as the months have passed, I believe that they were correct to do so.'

Petr paused, his eyes wide. 'You think… it was right

that I became leader?'

'It was.' She laughed again, a throaty, intimate laugh at odds with her austere reputation. 'Even the Dazai can make mistakes. She is merely the adviser, the sage, the ceremonial outpouring of that which is within… She is still human, and she is not beyond making mistakes!'

'You are very generous, noble Dazai,' said Petr. 'I wish I were so accepting of my past errors!'

'You know I would see you at any time,' continued the Dazai as they passed a group of men and women beating the rugs outside their homes. 'It is your right as elder, and my privilege as your subject.'

'I'm not… I'm not sure how I match up to my younger brother. I have none of his strength, his prowess, his bravery…'

'It is as I said: your qualities, your strength, are *different*. That does not imply worthlessness.'

'Sometimes I wish I was more like Saul,' said Petr. 'Nothing seems to bother him.'

'You know that isn't true,' said the Dazai. 'We are all affected. It is true that this shadow has not yet passed over Saul's family. That does not mean that he is indifferent to the suffering of others. None of us are.'

'Then you can understand why I wanted to speak with you,' said Petr. 'If Saul knows something, has some insight…'

'If Saul knew anything he would come to you.'

'I hope that's true.' Petr sighed. 'I hope… I'm doing

the right thing. Saul's urge to get help from beyond the village… He's not without his supporters, you know.'

'You must continue to do what you think is best,' said the Dazai as they came to a halt outside the ceremonial hall. Larger than any other building within the village, its pitched roof seemed to slice into the sky. Flags fluttered from its corner and metal lanterns clashed and chimed as they hung over the great doorway. 'As I have told you before, help will come, in one form or another,' continued the Dazai with a smile. 'It always does.'

Martha tugged desperately at the toothed trap that had snapped shut around the Doctor's ankle. He appeared not to have lost much blood – though he'd made some quip about needing to dry-clean his trousers later – and the rough metal jaws seemed not to have closed entirely, allowing him to move his leg a little. Despite this, he seemed to be – if that were possible – even more manic than usual. Martha reckoned it was some sort of shock kicking in – though goodness only knew what kind of shock an alien with two hearts might suffer.

'I must stop doing this!' said the Doctor, his eyes wide. 'It really is rather embarrassing.'

'It sounds like you make a habit of it.'

'Oh, you know, every few hundred years or so. And then there was this school trip…'

'You went on a school trip?'

'I use the term somewhat loosely. I mean, can you

imagine me sat at the back of a clapped-out old bus rolling stink bombs down the aisle and chatting up Lucy McGregor from class 6C?'

'Actually, I can,' said Martha.

The Doctor snorted. 'Oh, you've got such a low opinion of me, Martha Jones! My teachers thought I was a model pupil. I *never* got into trouble.' He paused. 'Well, not that often.' He glanced away. 'Well, not when it really mattered. Well, not on a day with a "z" in it, anyway...'

Suddenly his face broke into a broad grin. 'Oh, hello!' he said more loudly, looking over Martha's shoulder. 'Martha, we have company,' he added.

Martha turned. Coming towards them across the clearing was a tall, broad man in brown robes. His face was hard to read, though his eyes seemed to twinkle with energy. A sword – thankfully sheathed – glinted at his belt, and his long, wild-looking hair was pulled back into a pigtail. He was moving silently over the branches and leaf litter of the forest floor – and, disconcertingly, he wasn't even looking at the Doctor and Martha.

He bent down at the Doctor's feet and, without a word, flicked a hidden catch and pulled open the trap. He indicated, with an impatient move of his head, the far side of the clearing.

'Well, thank you,' said the Doctor, who seemed not to have noticed the man's anxious demeanour. 'I'm most grateful for your...'

The man hissed the Doctor into silence and gestured

at the other side of the clearing again. As Martha and the Doctor moved away – the Doctor was hobbling slightly but able to walk unaided – Martha saw the man, still crouching, draw his sword silently. The weapon was subtly curved, but short enough for use in the limited spaces afforded by the dense forest.

Throughout his encounter with the Doctor and Martha, the man's eyes had been fixed on something else, some deeper darkness between the trees, and only now did Martha see what had so transfixed and terrified him.

A vast, awkward creature had advanced on the Doctor and Martha while they'd been preoccupied with the trap. Though still largely obscured by foliage, Martha caught glimpses of its skin – hide? – as it moved from side to side as if assessing its targets. She glimpsed prominent, ridged bones, with eviscerated skin almost seeming to hang in strips, impossibly slender limbs, and, just once, scarlet eyes that burned with a malignant intelligence.

'Keep walking,' whispered the Doctor, who'd obviously seen the creature now. His voice was simple and serious, all trace of mania – and his usual humour – gone.

Their rescuer, too, was backing away, still almost on his haunches as if coiled to strike, still staring implacably at the huge, obscured beast. Only when the man came alongside the Doctor and Martha did he sheathe his sword and engage them in conversation. His voice was deep and warm but he spoke in clipped, anxious words.

'Do you need help?' he asked the Doctor. 'We need to get away from here.'

'I'm OK,' said the Doctor. 'Thanks for sorting out that trap.'

'Normally I am alone in the forest,' said the man, by way of apology.

'What was that creature?' asked Martha.

'Something that does not belong here,' said the man.

'And we're safe now?' asked Martha, risking a glance behind her. She couldn't see the clearing now, still less any sign of the tall, angular beast that had watched them through the trees.

'Let's hope so,' said the man, though he sounded less than certain.

The man, who introduced himself as Saul, quickly escorted the Doctor and Martha to the edge of the forest. He said little as they walked, his eyes and ears alert instead for any sign that the creature had followed them through the trees. Martha noticed that the birds were silent now; all she could hear were their own footsteps. Each step sounded impossibly loud; each twig that snapped underfoot was like a rifle shot.

The trees began to thin, the undergrowth becoming less ragged and more luxuriant. The Doctor kept trying to scan Saul with his sonic screwdriver, surreptitiously;

Martha glowered at him, worried that this would be construed as rudeness – or a provocation. But thankfully Saul's back was always turned to them.

Suddenly they were out in the open, standing high on a hillside, looking down on a lush valley of grass cut through by a twisting river. And, clustered on one bank of the river as it blossomed suddenly into an expansive lake, sat a village of flags and spired buildings.

'Home?' queried the Doctor.

Saul nodded. 'My brother did not tell me we were expecting visitors.' He turned back to the Doctor and Martha. 'I'm sorry if you're in pain,' he added ruefully, indicating the Doctor's ankle.

The Doctor waved away the apology. 'Your brother is?'

'Our elected leader. You'll want to speak to him first.'

They began to descend the hillside. Even from this distance Martha could see horses and cows in the fields and children playing outside a school. It was a comforting, everyday sight after their close encounter with the beast in the forest.

They followed a small dirt track into the village, Martha wondering idly if Saul had created this himself by sheer dint of having walked to and from the woods so often. And then she noticed that there was no proper road into the village at all. It seemed entirely cut off from the outside world.

And then she reminded herself that, as far as they

knew, they were still within, or attached to, the space station she and the Doctor had explored. Perhaps there was no 'outside world' – perhaps this was all there was. But the illusion of a far larger reality was persuasive. The mountains and rolling hills that framed the scene seemed utterly real. If this was merely some computer simulation, some painted backdrop, it was breathtakingly detailed.

Martha wondered – if she and the Doctor just carried on walking, would they eventually come to the edge of the world?

'I would very much like to see your brother,' said the Doctor suddenly, as if he'd come to some sort of decision. He stopped for a moment to look at Saul. 'I'm afraid I may have some… interesting news for him. For all of you…'

'Oh?'

'I don't know quite how to say this, but…' The Doctor sighed and glanced away. His manner reminded Martha of a hospital consultant about to deliver terrible news. 'The fact of the matter is, I'm pretty sure you, the mountains, the village…' He indicated the entire vista before them with his outstretched hand. 'None of this *existed* a couple of hours ago.'

FIVE

Jude was bored. The constant droning of the teacher's voice had become a lullaby designed only to make her eyelids feel heavier and heavier. She'd enjoyed the lesson about the history of the village, which, like a stone skipping over still water, had touched on everything from glaciers and how valleys are formed, to history and the lives of the first leaders of their community.

Now, however, mathematics was in full swing – or, rather, would have been, if only Mr Somo would let them all get on with the exercises he had set. Instead, the sour-faced teacher seemed intent on discussing the theory. He must have repeated the same point about twenty times now, and if Jude had once understood what Mr Somo was driving at, she was no longer quite so sure.

Jude let her mind wander back over the history lesson. It was somehow comforting to think that generations of children – doubtless many as bored as she was – had sat in this room and listened to teachers going on about the importance of mathematics in everyday life. Some had perhaps become elders or advisers; others, who history would never record, had led perfectly happy lives working in the fields and drinking in the inn. Jude wondered if these people should be venerated at least as much as the leaders of the past, for Jude's father had often said that deciding to concentrate on looking after a family – rather than meddling in the lives of the whole village – was an especially noble calling.

Jude let her fingers run over the rough surface of her desk. Names had been scratched into its surface with knives and the broken nibs of ink pens; she wondered idly if 'CB' was still in love with 'AR', and if 'Tomas J' still lived in the village, or had long since been consigned to the ground.

Jude thought a lot about death these days. She supposed that was normal enough – she'd be a teenager in a few months and her father had often warned her to be on her guard against 'depressing thoughts' as she got older. And, given what had happened lately, it was no surprise that the entire village seemed less lively than usual. Of course, everybody knew that death was a normal part of life, like night-time as a necessary opposite to day, but Jude had found herself dwelling on such things recently.

This morning there had been another empty desk in the schoolroom. Jude didn't really know Farah all that well, but Sayan had said that Farah's mother had been up since daybreak, searching the village, eyes raw and red with crying. The other children had tried to ignore the empty desk, but Jude kept looking over at it, still shocked by everyone's resigned acceptance. Jude couldn't just *accept* what had happened; she didn't understand what caused the children to disappear, but she knew, somehow, that it must be fought against. It must be resisted, not given in to.

One window looked out towards the lake and its small island. Farah had played on the shore only yesterday, orchestrating some of the younger children into a game of catchball. She'd laughed when the mist seemed to roll off the surface of the lake and onto the fields, running through the fog and flapping her arms in defiance and laughter.

And now the fog had taken her…

Or had it?

Jude blinked, rubbing her eyes. Wasn't there someone out there now? A dark form, its humanity stripped away by the obscuring grey haze, until it resembled little more than a child's stick drawing flailing in the mist. It was probably nothing, some adult taking a shortcut behind the school on their way home.

Suddenly the fog parted, and Jude almost cried out in surprise. She continued to stare, ignoring everything around her, paying no heed to the icicle fingers that were now running up and down her spine.

Farah stood outside, drained of colour, seemingly drained of life, staring at the school with grim, uncomprehending fascination. Even her clothes, which suddenly seemed to hang from her pale, thin body, appeared as if bleached and drained of all vibrancy.

'Jude, are you paying attention?'

Jude snapped her head back into the classroom. Mr Somo was standing over her, his face screwed up in irritation, a vein at the side of his head pulsing slowly.

'Sir, it's…'

Jude looked back towards the lake. In a moment, the fog seemed to have receded, leaving a pristine field of grass that cried out for children to play over it. Of the pale figure there was absolutely no sign.

'What?' Somo's face leaned ever closer.

Jude shook her head, concerned – but aware that her own troubles were only just beginning if she couldn't placate Mr Somo.

'Sorry, sir… Just daydreaming.'

'Perhaps a little extra homework would help you focus on the task at hand?' Mr Somo stood staring for a few moments more, then returned to his position at the front of the class. 'If you could all now begin the exercise in front of you…'

As Jude began to write she risked one last glance through the window.

There was no one there.

* * *

They walked into the village in silence. Martha wasn't sure if in some strange way they had offended Saul, or if he now simply considered them mad and was giving them a wide berth.

As they approached the large, ceremonial building that dominated one end of the central green, the Doctor nudged Martha in the ribs. 'What do you make of this place?' he whispered.

'Odd,' said Martha, still struggling with the implications of what the Doctor had said to Saul. 'I don't see a supermarket or a fast food place anywhere,' she added, trying to make light of the situation.

'All right, given that,' said the Doctor, patiently, 'what do you think of its architecture, its style, its culture... In Earth terms, does it suggest anything at all?'

Martha looked around, trying to take it all in. 'Well, I suppose... I don't know really... Tibet?'

'A mishmash of influences from Earth,' said the Doctor. 'All jumbled together, along with stuff I'm not sure I recognise – sliding doors in frames shaped like keyholes, triangular windows...' He pointed to the green square of grass at the centre of the village; the children were playing some complex game with bats and balls, under the watchful eye of a trader who'd set up a stall. 'Look at that quickly and you'd think we were in the Cotswolds, look back at those mountains and you'd swear we were in the Andes.'

'What's your point?'

'I'm not sure,' admitted the Doctor. He glanced at Saul, some feet ahead of them. He gave no sign of listening in on their conversation, though he did glance over his shoulder from time to time to check they were still there.

'Another thing,' continued the Doctor. 'This place seems absolutely isolated, and yet… No one's staring at us. No one's suspicious or frightened. I haven't even flashed the old psychic paper yet!' He drummed his fingers against his cheeks, thinking out loud. 'S'ppose it explains one thing, though,' he said.

'What?'

'That big jumble of readings we got back on the *Castor*,' said the Doctor. 'It's not one creature, but hundreds – every person in the village, every cow in the field, every bear in the forest – all rolled into one. No wonder the poor computer couldn't make sense of it!'

'What you said about this place not really existing,' said Martha. 'Do you mean that?'

'Did we see a chunk of planet on the TARDIS scanners when we looked at the research centre?' reasoned the Doctor. 'Was any of this here when we first explored?'

'We could be the ones who are mistaken,' said Martha. 'I mean, the TARDIS is bigger on the inside than the outside. Why not a spaceship that works the same way?'

'Lots of reasons,' said the Doctor. 'And when you open the outer door, the control room is always there.'

He paused. 'Well, nine times out of ten,' he added in a whisper.

'Sorry?'

'The inside of the TARDIS,' said the Doctor more loudly. 'It isn't switched on and off like a light in a fridge.'

'And this place was?'

'Seems that way,' said the Doctor. 'We left the TARDIS in a deserted corridor, and returned to find a door leading to a forest. Draw your own conclusions!'

'But this seems so real,' said Martha. 'We've walked for miles. I can smell someone cooking dinner. That man over there is repairing the tiles on his roof...'

'Dreams seem real enough, when you're asleep.'

'Dreams don't seem to have real people in them, going about their lives. I just think we should tread carefully, that's all.'

The Doctor nodded slowly. He seemed intrigued by her reaction. It was as if, from time to time, he needed a compass to live his life by – and a human one at that.

Moments later they stopped outside the ceremonial building at the heart of the village. Saul began to ascend the steps.

'Wait here,' he said. 'I will tell Petr that you have arrived.'

'So,' said Petr, settling down in a vast wooden chair and indicating that the Doctor and Martha should also sit. 'My brother tells me you don't think any of us exist?'

'No, I don't mean that,' said the Doctor, trying to be diplomatic. 'But I'm pretty sure none of this…' With a broad wave of his hands he indicated the meeting room, the building itself, the village beyond. 'None of this existed earlier today.'

The leader seemed amused rather than outraged. He was a tall man, not as well built as Saul, but wiry and supple. He had piercing eyes and a pronounced Adam's apple that bobbed as he spoke, as if underlining the importance of his words. If he was disturbed by the very thought of his own unreality, he was doing a good job of hiding it.

He leant forward to look at the Doctor more closely, absent-mindedly running a hand through his dark, unruly hair. 'And yet we clearly exist now, or you would not waste your time talking to us. What is your evidence for this startling claim…?'

The Doctor sighed. 'It's hard to explain. You'll have to trust us.'

'Forgive me if I *don't*,' said Petr. 'We have lived in this valley for hundreds of years. We have written records going back to the first elected leader, and beyond. We rise each morning, we eat and sleep, we have physical form… And yet, today, a stranger turns up, denying our very reality! Is this some sort of trick, or are you merely mad, sir?'

'All I'm saying is – you can't believe everything you see.'

Petr laughed. 'At last we have some common ground!

We can both, I think, agree on that.' He leaned forward. 'And your friend?' he said, looking to Martha. 'What does she say?'

Martha cleared her throat. 'Well, um… We were on this… ship in the stars… We were trying to return to our own… craft. We were walking down this corridor when… all of this appeared.'

'Then at least it is a shared madness,' said Petr, a note of disappointment in his voice. The man's tone surprised Martha – it was as if, beneath that unflappable exterior, he had expected more of the Doctor and Martha. Petr got to his feet. 'Now, forgive me, I have more urgent matters to consider…'

'Look, sorry to be nosy,' said the Doctor, 'but can I ask what these "urgent matters" are?'

Petr stared back at the Doctor, his face thoughtful. 'Some people have disappeared from the village,' he said eventually. 'Always children. Always at night.'

'Do these kids know each other?' asked Martha. In her experience, children were always running away from home – or threatening to. But for a group of them to disappear, and not return – and in as enclosed a community as this – clearly spoke of something more sinister.

Petr shook his head. 'It seems random, a…' He paused before proceeding, his eyes distant. 'It is a different family every time. It is as if some… dark angel passes over our homes at night.'

'And how often has this happened?' asked the Doctor.

'Eight times,' said Petr. 'But the attacks are getting more frequent.'

'Any evidence?' queried Martha. 'Broken doors or windows, that sort of thing…?'

Another shake of the head. 'Windows and doors are still locked. The beds seem… undisturbed.'

For the first time Petr's voice cracked with emotion, and Martha could see the impact this was having on him. Small wonder he wasn't really taking the Doctor seriously – his mind was on other things.

'Now, I must go and speak with the latest family,' said Petr abruptly. 'I must assure them that we are doing all that we can. But in truth… it was a mystery when the first child vanished, and it remains a mystery now.'

'What's the name of this village?' said the Doctor, changing tack suddenly.

Petr looked puzzled, as if he barely understood the question. 'It's our home, where we live – and where we have always lived…'

'But surely,' continued the Doctor, 'this place must have a name? On the way over, your brother told me that you sometimes welcome travellers and traders. If you were to write a formal document on behalf of the village, how would you describe yourself? Elder of…?'

'I am the twelfth elected elder of Herot.'

'Herot? That sounds like… How interesting!' said the Doctor breathlessly.

'Interesting?' queried Martha.

'I'll tell you later,' whispered the Doctor, turning once more back to Petr. 'Tell me about your contact with the outside world. What region are we in? What land, what country, what nation? Who rules over you, who do you have treaties with?'

'Our allegiance is only to each other, to the life we wish to live in peace. As for wider, worldly matters… I cannot answer your questions. They do not concern us.' Petr looked closely at the Doctor. 'If you hail from these distant regions, you yourself must know the answers to your questions.'

'Could I have a look at these documents you mentioned?' asked the Doctor.

'Of course,' said Petr. 'I am glad to welcome you both to our village,' he said as he got to his feet. 'I think you will provide… entertainment, if nothing else. A distraction from our very real worries.'

Martha left the Doctor examining the records kept in the ceremonial hall. Apparently the most recent documents were stored there, while much older records were looked after by the Dazai, some sort of sage who lived on the edge of the village. The Doctor had said he was going to visit her later – after a quick detour in the general direction of the village pub.

Petr's wife, Kristine, had walked into the room and introduced herself, somewhat uncertainly, and then accompanied Martha back to their home. As personal guests of the leader, the Doctor and Martha would have the most lavish rooms the village could offer.

Such things are, of course, relative. As Martha sat on the edge of a large bed in an almost bare room she resisted the temptation to look under the downy blanket for fleas or goodness knows what. It wasn't exactly five star, she concluded, but the villagers clearly meant well.

There was a tall canvas cupboard in one corner, and a simple wooden table, complete with jug of water, by the window. The window itself afforded a fine view of the bustling centre of the village. Martha watched as people went about their business: an old man with a stick, bowing low as he passed a couple of young women in brightly coloured dresses; a lad in his late teens reading a book as he leant against the sun-drenched side of a house; women – and men – haggling over prices in the market. From somewhere there came the sound of music – a sitar or some equivalent. It *had* to be real – but what link could all this possibly have to the space station with its dead bodies and its sinister, oppressive atmosphere?

Martha still thought some sort of portal was the most likely explanation for everything that had happened – that she and the Doctor had stepped through from one area of space and time to another – but then, unbidden, the memory of the metallic tree came to mind. It was as if the space station had *merged* into the forest and everything that was beyond it.

Martha walked out of the bedroom, descended the stairs, and saw Kristine hanging out the washing on a line at the back of the house. Kristine was a dark, broad woman, and beads of sweat were just appearing on her forehead as she worked her way efficiently through a large basket of clothing.

Martha walked through the open door and out into the yard. Kristine turned as she heard Martha approach. 'Is your room… appropriate?' she asked, bowing low. 'I'm not sure what you are used to.'

Martha seized on the comment, wondering if what Petr had said could possibly be true – that they really did have almost no contact with any other settlement. 'What do you know about the outside world?' she queried.

'Nothing,' Kristine said simply. 'We keep ourselves to ourselves.'

'But people visit you from nearby towns,' persisted Martha. 'There must be travellers, traders…'

'Oh yes,' said Kristine. 'Once in a while we see people from beyond the village. They stay with us for a few hours, a few days, and then they leave.'

'Has any villager ever travelled to one of these towns?'

Kristine shook her head. 'Even Saul has never ventured beyond the forest.'

'Why not?'

'Because my brother has said that I should not,' said Saul, stepping out of the house and towards the two women.

'And you always do what your brother tells you?' said Martha, turning. It was a genuine question but it came out sounding a little more sarcastic than she had meant.

Saul paused for a moment, momentarily taken aback. 'Of course I do… He is our elected leader.' He turned to Kristine. 'I was only able to check half the traps this morning. I'm going back to the woods now.'

'Don't worry, Saul,' said Kristine, resting a hand on his arm. 'I have some salted meat put aside.'

Saul moved away from Kristine, embarrassed by her physical contact. Martha saw a brief look pass between them.

Saul shook his head. 'I said I'd bring something fresh, and that's what I intend to do. Even your skill cannot turn stale ingredients into a banquet!'

Kristine turned to Martha. 'A long-standing arrangement,' she explained. 'Petr and Saul have not seen much of each other for some months.' She performed another half-bow in Martha's direction. 'You would, of course, be more than welcome to come.'

'Thanks.' Martha turned to Saul. 'Do you mind if I tag along? I need to stretch my legs…' In truth, Martha remained convinced that there was more to the forest than met the eye, but she wasn't about to tell Saul that.

Saul looked Martha up and down, as if assessing her suitability to be a companion on his trip. 'All right,' he said at last. 'We'll meet over by the lake. I need to get some things first.'

He bowed to both women, and then was gone. Kristine continued to stare into the middle distance, a distracted look on her face.

'Petr told us about the missing children,' said Martha quietly. 'A terrible thing to have happened.'

Kristine managed a weak smile. 'We lost Thom a month ago. Our only child. I suppose it means we can share in the sadness of the others, but even so...' She glanced downward, perhaps wanting to hide the extent of her emotion from Martha. 'All I want is for Thom to come back.'

'Of course you do,' said Martha. 'I'm sorry, I had no idea...'

'You don't understand,' said Kristine sharply. 'It's wrong for me to want to see Thom again!'

'I'm sure it's perfectly natural...'

'No.' Kristine looked up, tears softening her features. 'If Thom, if the other departed children, return to us... Then the village will be destroyed.'

SIX

The Doctor stood before the little house at the edge of the village. Before he could even knock, the door slid back, as if the old woman had been standing there, listening for his arrival.

She was stooped and her skin was cracked and folded, but her eyes were bright and they danced continuously, as if trying to make sense of this strange man standing on her doorstep.

'Hello,' said the Doctor brightly. 'I've got some questions about the history of the village. I'm told you're the person to speak to.'

'Ah,' said the woman. 'You're the man who thinks we're all a figment of someone else's imagination.' She smiled, a rictus of dry lips and crooked teeth.

'Blimey,' said the Doctor, his face falling. 'Word travels fast around here, doesn't it?'

'People who don't really exist obviously have little

else to talk about,' said the woman, her voice rich with sarcasm.

'I said you *didn't* exist,' said the Doctor. 'It's perfectly clear that you do *now*.' He paused. 'At least, I think that's what I said. It's a complicated situation…'

'Are we real?' demanded the woman firmly, 'or are *you* the phantasm, a wandering spirit designed to unsettle us all…? As if we don't already have troubles enough,' added the woman more quietly.

'I thought I was supposed to ask *you* the questions,' said the Doctor after a pause.

The woman smiled again. 'Come in,' she said, moving aside so the Doctor could enter. 'I will make some tea.'

'Of course,' said the Doctor, relieved. 'I find metaphysical questions much easier to handle over a nice cuppa…'

Kristine refused to say anything else about her son and disappeared back inside the house. Martha was left in the cool afternoon sunshine, wondering if there was some way she could comfort Kristine, or if she should just follow her instinct and go back into the forest with Saul.

She sighed, and headed in the direction of the lake, wondering if facing monsters in the woods was somehow easier than aiding a grieving mother.

As she walked, she turned Kristine's words over in her mind. How could the return of these poor kids be linked to the destruction of the village? If they weren't dead, if they hadn't been murdered – and Petr had indicated that all the children had simply 'disappeared' – then where had they gone?

Martha found Saul standing by the lake, talking to a bright-eyed girl who must have been about twelve. It seemed that school had finished for the day as other children were spilling out from their classrooms, delighted by their long-promised liberation. The girl seemed rather serious for her age, addressing Saul confidently. Martha caught a little of their conversation before both became aware of her presence.

'You know as well as I do,' said the girl. 'The legends about the island and the fog… They're absolutely clear!'

'And I'm not a great believer in legends,' said Saul. 'Things I can see and touch… That's all I'm interested in.'

'Normally I'd agree with you,' said the girl. 'But the coincidence of it all! First the disappearances, and then Farah coming back…'

'You're mistaken,' said Saul gruffly. 'Your friend Farah will not be returning. I'm sorry.'

At that moment they heard Martha approach and turned. Saul beamed, wrapping a huge arm around the girl's shoulders as though nothing was the matter.

'This is Jude,' he explained. 'My daughter.'

'I think I'll come with you,' announced the girl, shaking herself free of Saul's embrace and obviously still spoiling for a fight with her father. 'I haven't been up in the woods for *ages*!'

'Not today,' said Saul, a low, warning note in his voice. 'You know you're not supposed to go there at all.'

'Oh, father, don't be silly! It's not like I'm asking to go to the *island* or anything. It's perfectly safe.'

'*No*,' said Saul, even more firmly. 'Sorry.'

Jude was about to continue the debate but obviously caught the stern look in her father's eyes. 'See you later,' she said with a frustrated sigh before bowing to Martha and turning away. She wasn't exactly in a strop, but it was clear to Martha that she wasn't best pleased either.

Saul watched her go, parental concern clear on his strong features.

'Kids, eh?' said Martha, trying to lighten the mood.

'You have children of your own?' asked Saul, looking her up and down. 'Babies, perhaps,' he added hurriedly, as if to avoid causing offence.

'No, no,' said Martha hurriedly. 'But I've got a family. Mum, dad, sister and brother. Amounts to the same thing.'

They started to ascend the hill towards the dark slab of trees.

'You want to protect your daughter from the monsters,' said Martha. 'That's understandable.'

Saul glanced over his shoulder at the receding buildings. 'But if the village is no longer safe…'

'Kristine told me about the children who've gone

missing,' said Martha. 'She mentioned some sort of legend, but wouldn't say anything else about it.'

'You should talk to the Dazai,' said Saul. 'She knows of such things.'

'That sounds like the Doctor's territory,' said Martha. 'I think he's on his way to see her.'

Saul smiled. 'Two very strong wills… I imagine they'll get on well,' he said.

Soon Martha was back under the canopy of leaves at the forest's edge. She wasn't quite sure what she was hoping to find, though she supposed some trace of the research vessel *Castor* was quite high on the list. The station meant a link to the TARDIS, and the TARDIS meant home. There was an uncomfortable feeling in the pit of Martha's stomach; it reminded her of the panic that had gripped her on one package holiday to Ibiza when she thought she'd lost her passport and tickets in a bar and – ridiculous though it later sounded – wondered if she'd ever see London again.

In the shady tranquillity of the trees, Saul proved as matter-of-fact as the Doctor had been delighted and intrigued. He said little of consequence as they ventured deeper, beyond identifying occasional birds from their trilling calls and showing Martha the muddy tracks of some bear-like creature. She still thought the forest was magical. She didn't understand why or how any of it was here, but she appreciated its haunting beauty well enough.

A bit like life, she supposed.

Moments later, Saul bent down to concentrate on one of a series of metal traps, smaller equivalents of the device that had snapped shut around the Doctor's ankle. He cracked open the metal jaws, and pulled out a blood-streaked rabbit. He hooked the creature onto his belt and reset the trap.

'Your friend recovered very quickly,' said Saul, not looking up.

'He's amazing,' said Martha, remembering her first proper meeting with the Doctor, and the surprise she'd got when she'd heard *two* beating hearts through her stethoscope. 'For all I know, you can chop off his arm and he'll grow a new one.'

'That's handy,' said Saul, keeping a straight face.

Martha thought back to the creature in the clearing. 'This morning… I suppose we were making a bit of a racket. It must have attracted that monster we saw.'

Saul frowned. 'I suppose.'

'What then?' asked Martha, picking up on the uncertainty in his voice.

Saul looked up, as if suspicious that the forest could hear their words. 'You asked me earlier why I don't travel beyond the woods,' said Saul, standing and wiping his bloodstained hands on his trousers. 'The thing is, I am the only one in the village who even shows any *interest* in going further. The others… They seem satisfied to just stay put. I don't suppose they share my desire to explore.'

'Life in the village has never been enough for you,' observed Martha.

Saul nodded. 'I'm content enough. I have a daughter and a wife and I love them both dearly. But I'm happiest if I'm moving, if I'm doing something.' He looked around him again, as if the forest were suddenly alive – and something to be feared. 'I told you I respected my brother's wishes, and that's true. But… Once or twice… I have tried to go beyond the edge of the forest. I want to see what happens when my maps run out…'

Martha smiled. 'Here be monsters,' she said, remembering the ancient maps from Earth history that indicated all manner of dragons and beasts at their uncharted extremities.

'That's it,' said Saul, nodding. 'That's exactly what holds me back.'

'Monsters?'

'Like the thing we saw. And worse… I can guarantee if you keeping heading north from here, that's what you'll see.'

'Monsters, guarding the edges of your world,' said Martha, thinking aloud. She pointed towards the mountains and to the area just south of the village where grassland began to merge into stonier terrain. 'And in that direction?'

'The same,' commented Saul. 'I've tried walking in every direction – and each time I've returned, my tail between my legs. A coward.' He bowed his head, ashamed.

'If I were you, Saul, I'd run a mile from these things as well.'

'I don't *know* that the creatures are dangerous,' continued Saul.

'The one we saw didn't look exactly friendly,' said Martha. 'How do traders get through?'

Saul shrugged. If the unexplored and distant mountains didn't really exist, Martha supposed, then perhaps the visitors were also entirely unreal.

'Everyone else just accepts these things,' said Saul. 'No one ever ventures into the forest, we are barred from the island in the lake… It never occurs to anyone to ask why this is.'

'Apart from your daughter.'

Saul nodded, sheepishly.

'What about your brother?' queried Martha. 'He seems bright enough.'

'If such things trouble him he has never told me,' said Saul simply. 'I had thought, when Thom went missing… Perhaps it would make Petr less cautious.' Saul sighed. 'It's just made him even worse. Soon I wonder if I'll even be allowed in the forest.'

'You think Petr will stop you coming up here?'

'Perhaps,' said Saul. 'Perhaps it will be too dangerous by then anyway. When I first saw that creature watching you and the Doctor in the clearing… I was deeply troubled. I had never seen one of the monsters in that part of the forest before.'

'They're getting closer to the village?'

Saul looked around, sensitive to the very air as it gusted and moved around him. He seemed on edge now, bent close to the ground, coiled as if to strike.

'Saul?' queried Martha, concerned.

'I think we're being watched,' he said in a low whisper.

The Doctor settled down at the Dazai's table. 'I popped into your local earlier,' he said, gratefully accepting the tea she offered. 'I was expecting a sudden hush, an anxious barman offering me a jug of ale... Suspicion and dread.'

'And instead you found...?'

'Tiredness,' said the Doctor. 'Resignation. Indifference.'

'It is not yet evening,' said the Dazai. 'I am told that things are... more exciting... later in the day.'

'Really?' said the Doctor. He took a sip of the tea. 'Anyway, they all agreed you were the woman I must speak to.'

'Ah,' said the Dazai. 'My... reputation.'

'Which is?'

'A source of wisdom – though not the only one, lest you accuse me of arrogance.' She smiled. 'The Dazai is an honorary title, passed on from mother to daughter in an endless cycle. At least, that's what most people think...'

'And others?'

'Rumours abound that I am the only Dazai, and that I have been here since the creation of all things.'

The Doctor laughed. 'Oh, go on. You don't look a day over fifty to me!'

'Flatterer,' said the Dazai. 'You think you can make your talk sweet, and then convince me of the falseness of our lives?'

'You reckon that's why I'm here?' asked the Doctor.

'I know I must learn from all who pass through our village,' said the Dazai. 'And, perhaps, be of benefit to them, too. The truth, Doctor – do we exist, or not? Are we real?'

The Doctor sighed. 'Depends what you mean, I suppose,' he said.

'Even if you could convince me,' said the old woman, watching the Doctor closely as he sipped at his tea, 'I am not sure it makes very much difference to the conversation we are having. There are some that say we are *all* but the dreams of God.' She grinned, and the Doctor saw immediately the intelligence that animated her features. 'Can you prove to me *you* are not the expression of some higher life force, some other entity or vast cosmic machine…?'

'That *is* a tricky one,' said the Doctor, puffing his cheeks. 'I can only really tell you what I've seen – that I'm pretty sure none of this was here earlier, that it all came into being just like *that*…' He clicked his fingers.

'By our own eyes – by the evidence of our senses – we *create* the universe,' said the Dazai. 'Even if, by science, we think we can make some statement about the age of the universe… It makes no difference to any one of us as an individual. When we sleep, it is as if the universe blinks out of existence.'

'*Cogito ergo sum,*' said the Doctor. 'I'm thinking, therefore I exist. Yes, that's a very interesting way of putting it.'

'But you did not come here to debate philosophy,' said the Dazai, suddenly getting to her feet and shuffling to the rear of the room. There, stretching from floor almost to ceiling and very nearly as wide as the room, was a great wooden bookcase, blackened with age and use. On it were row upon row of leather-backed books, each spine lined with golden lettering and fitting snugly against its neighbour. 'The history of our people,' said the old woman. 'One of the roles of the Dazai is to record all events of great importance.'

The Doctor whistled, amazed at the sheer number of volumes before him. 'Births, marriages, deaths…?'

'That, and more,' said the Dazai. 'Every meeting, every decision…'

The Doctor selected a book at random. 'Do you mind…?'

The Dazai shook her head. 'Go ahead. See the true extent of our history.'

The Doctor tugged the book from the shelf, pulled it

open, and saw page upon page of notes and annotations. Different inks, different standards of neatness, even – every now and again – entirely different handwriting. 'Fascinating!' he exclaimed. 'Quite fascinating.' He flicked through the book quickly, a blur of parchment and ink, then paused, examining the book from numerous angles as if expecting it to explode at any minute. 'You have many meetings, then?' he asked.

'You'd be surprised,' said the Dazai with a smile.

'It's just… A little place like this, no links to the outside world, seemingly no big dilemmas or problems… What on Earth do your leaders talk about all day?'

The Dazai said nothing and, just for a moment, the Doctor wondered if she'd gently encouraged him to ask these questions, with a view to ending up at this position. It was entirely possible that the Dazai was driving the discussion, manipulating the Doctor into thinking that *he* was the one in the driving seat.

He grabbed another book from the shelf, opened it, flicked through its pages – more of the same. Amongst the prosaic details he found frequent mentions of the woods that surrounded the village, the fog that came across the lake – and the forbidden island at its heart. 'Would I be right in thinking,' he said, casually, 'that something *is* going on at the moment? That there is some sort of problem…?'

'Why do you say that?' asked the Dazai.

'Petr told me about the missing children,' said the

Doctor. 'Anyway, call it bad luck, but when I arrive somewhere… Within five minutes it's monsters and life 'n' death and *chaos*, guaranteed.'

'Do you precipitate this chaos, or are you merely drawn to it?'

'I do wonder sometimes,' said the Doctor, snapping the book shut and replacing it on the shelves. 'People say you cannot measure something or observe it without altering it in some way…'

'And by your very arrival you might inadvertently cause some change in your environment?'

'Either that,' admitted the Doctor, pulling another book at random from the shelves, 'or the TARDIS has a real nose for trouble.'

'TARDIS?'

'My… ship. It's thanks to the TARDIS that we're…' His voice trailed away to nothing.

'Is there a problem, Doctor?' asked the Dazai.

The pages within the volume the Doctor was inspecting were entirely blank. He returned it carefully to its place on the shelf, extracted another book. This one had a few pages of writing towards the back, but otherwise seemed unmarked. A third pulled from its place on the shelves was also empty – until, as the Doctor stared at the page, words began to appear, lines of dark pigment spreading across the surface of the parchment.

'No,' he said slowly, rubbing his eyes. 'No problem at all.'

SEVEN

Saul nodded towards an expanse of shadowed leaves. Branches were shaking; the undergrowth was crackling as if on fire. Something was coming closer and closer.

Martha risked another sideways glance at Saul. Crouching even lower to the ground, his face a mask of concentration, he had his elegant, short sword in his hand – Martha hadn't even heard him draw it from his scabbard – and was staring intently at the low bushes. Martha could hear twigs snapping now, whole branches kicked aside – there was no stealth or subtlety here.

The thing – whatever it was – was shrieking, a high-pitched whine that set Martha's teeth on edge.

She was just about to turn to Saul once more when the creature *exploded* out of the bush in a confusion of noise and scattered leaves.

It was like the animal that had disturbed her and the

Doctor earlier. Martha glimpsed a bristly brown hide, a gaping mouth full of spittle and tusks, and black-button eyes now wide with fear.

Martha almost laughed with relief, only now aware of her racing pulse and the weight of her heart as it thumped like an industrial piston in her chest.

She turned to Saul. 'We saw one of these earlier. I thought it was…'

Then she saw that Saul's countenance had not changed. He was making some impatient sideways motion with his head, still staring deep into the trees. It took a moment for Martha to understand what he meant, and then it hit her like a runaway bus. *The monster's still there.*

The creature announced its presence with a long, drawn-out cry, like a lamb's bleat filtered through a huge but broken megaphone. A sapling came crashing to the ground in a splash of silver trunk and mud-coloured leaves. Finally, through a forced break in the trees, a great, purplish creature staggered into the light. A vile, oozing body sat atop several great, twitching legs, multi-jointed like an insect's but as thick as an elephant's. Stunted wings covered with barbs and pustules flapped into the surrounding trees, breaking them effortlessly. Martha had to crane her head upwards to see the head, which swayed from side to side atop a sinuous, tapering neck. The 'face' was flattened vertically, resembling the jaws of a Venus flytrap, edged by lidless black eyes.

The creature lurched forward, its scimitar-shaped wing casings slicing another tree asunder. Everything it touched ran with blue and brown slime and the stench that rose from its bloated body was almost overpowering.

'What is that thing?' hissed Martha, terrified.

Saul, as stoic and controlled as ever, shook his head in disbelief.

Martha and Saul edged backwards, still watching the beast intently. One of its wings powered into the soil and leaves at their feet, but they jumped out the way easily. A warning shot.

'I've never encountered one this close to the village,' said Saul under his breath. He was clearly shocked by what he saw.

The beast rocked its head backwards, its circle of eyes now looking upwards, and let forth another reverberating cry.

'Come on,' said Saul, grabbing Martha by the arm. 'The forest is thicker over here. It won't be able to follow us.'

They plunged headlong into a grove of overlapping trees. Even the space between trunks and criss-crossing branches, it seemed, was filled with vines, creepers, brambles. It all became a blur as they ran, forcing their way through the dense vegetation. Martha was painfully aware of the knotted undergrowth that tugged at her feet and the sinuous woody stems that slapped into her face and arms. At one point she glanced down at her hands, exposed and unprotected, and saw that they were already red and raw.

But none of this mattered if it meant they were escaping from the creature. She could hear it thundering behind them, pressing its bulk against the wall of trees and brambles, crying out in frustration and defiance. Then, mercifully, after a time, the noises began to dwindle, and Martha and Saul slowed, moving the larger branches and trailing vines out of their way instead of just blundering into them. Eventually the trees began to thin, becoming, once more, larger and more majestic, until eventually they were back in a more familiar expanse of forest. Sunlight filtered through the canopy like great golden planks, seeming almost as solid as the trees that surrounded them.

Saul looked around, getting his bearings and sniffing the air, and then headed off. 'We should speak with the Doctor,' he said.

Martha nodded, folding her arms so that she didn't have to look at her throbbing and tender hands. Just at the moment she couldn't think of a single thing she wanted more than to see the Doctor again.

Word had gone around the school that morning that some travellers had been seen in the village. It was said they were staying at leader Petr's house, and their purpose in the village had soon become the subject of playground gossip. One boy had suggested that they were professional monster-killers, and another speculated that they were here to investigate the children who had gone missing. Soon, however, even Jude's friends had tired of this interruption to normal life in the village. The boys had wanted to play a rough sport of their own invention that seemed to involve ball-throwing and copious amounts of mud, but the girls were only interested in their own forfeit game of truth and kisses. Jude thought them equally pathetic and had been attracted to neither game – not when there were much more interesting things to occupy her mind.

After school, having unsuccessfully tried to accompany the female stranger and her father on a trip into the woods, Jude's thoughts had turned to tracking down the other newcomer. On discovering that he wasn't at the great hall or at uncle Petr's house, she guessed – rightly – that the wise woman would be his next port of call. She hid outside the Dazai's house, listening to their discussion and trying to follow as much of it as she could. Then, when the man – the Doctor, he called himself – had finished, Jude slipped out of the shadows and followed him.

The Doctor wandered through the village for some minutes, walking idly and taking a most circuitous route towards the lake. It was almost dark by the time he came to the water's edge. He sighed, as if disappointed – perhaps he had arranged to meet his friend and Jude's father there. Jude watched the stranger as he crouched down; he seemed to be looking intently at the stones at his feet, though he would glance up from time to time to stare across the grey expanse of water as if expecting to see something emerge from its depths.

Suddenly he started scrabbling around on the stony foreshore. Jude chose that moment to step out from her hiding place. 'Is everything all right?' she asked.

'Hello!' said the Doctor brightly, still scrabbling through the rocks. He made no attempt to ask Jude her name, or to question what she was doing there, or to tell her to go away. Jude liked the man already.

'What are you doing?' she continued.

'Ducks and Drakes!' said the Doctor, getting to his feet to show Jude the contents of his outstretched hands. 'You need a nice, flattish stone, a still expanse of water… It helps me to think.'

He paused, tongue locked between his teeth in concentration, then bent down, hurling the stone edgeways through the air and in the direction of the shrouded island. The stone skipped and bounced and arced across the water before eventually disappearing into the depths of the lake.

'Six jumps,' the Doctor breathed, counting the ripples. 'Not bad!'

'Oh, we call that *Skipping Circles*,' said Jude dismissively. 'A child's game. I've never seen the point in it.'

'Oh,' said the Doctor, crestfallen. 'Used to think it was wonderful when I was a kid…'

'Then, forgive me,' said Jude, 'but you must have been a bit, well, *dense*.'

The Doctor simply grinned. 'Oh yeah! Thicky thicky thick pants, that was me…'

'I'm not sure I believe you,' said Jude, with a disarming smile. 'You must be very wise, to have travelled so far.'

'Aw, thanks,' said the Doctor modestly. 'I matured quite late, you see,' he elaborated with an expansive hand gesture. 'Like a fine wine…'

'Or a smelly cheese,' suggested Jude, laughing.

'Gorgonzola!' exclaimed the Doctor, wrapping his lips around every syllable. 'I love a bit of Gorgonzola. Camembert, too. Do you know, I once bought some Brie from a village in Normandy and left it in a cupboard in the TARDIS… It was months and months before I found it again. You wouldn't believe the pong!'

'You're funny,' said Jude. 'Are you some sort of jester, a trickster from a foreign court? I've read about them in one of my books.'

'History?' queried the Doctor, sending another flat stone skipping over the water.

'Fiction,' said Jude. 'My father says there are only so many books full of long words you should read before you're twenty. I like to relax from time to time. Something… What's the word? Something *flippant*.'

'I like to relax by throwing stones,' said the Doctor firmly. 'Can't beat it. Who is your father…?'

'Saul,' said Jude.

'Ah,' said the Doctor. 'Why am I not surprised to hear that? While your dad tries to push back the barriers by exploring, you're trying to do the same – by reading loads of books!'

'Your friend went off with him to explore,' said Jude. 'I know he wanted to check his traps, but… That's sometimes code for "I fancy a bit of exploring today – don't tell anyone." He needs his peace and quiet, you see.'

'Martha went with him?' asked the Doctor, suddenly concerned.

'Oh, don't worry, she'll be quite safe.' Jude pointed to a pathway that wound towards the side of the village furthest from the forest. It was just starting to get dark now and the two figures were illuminated by a single guttering torch. 'Look, there they are!'

Jude waved at the taller of the two figures, then waited patiently alongside the Doctor. The silence as the evening darkened still further was interrupted as he threw another stone over the water.

It was impossible to count the number of skips now. The lake had become a mirror of the star-filled heavens, the stone seeming to fracture the night sky before sinking down into nothingness.

Martha came over to the Doctor in a rush, clearly out of breath and covered in scratches. 'Doctor,' she said hurriedly. 'We've seen a monster. In the forest. Like something out of Salvador Dalí.' Martha paused, trying to steady herself. 'Saul reckons there's loads of them. They're getting closer to the village.'

'Are you OK?' asked the Doctor.

'I'm fine,' said Martha. 'Though if I'd been in there on my own…'

The Doctor turned to Saul. 'Thank you,' he said simply. Saul bowed silently. The Doctor turned Martha away and whispered urgently to her. Jude had to strain to hear his words.

'It's just struck me,' the Doctor whispered. 'Those monsters might be the least of our problems…'

Martha and the Doctor walked back to Petr's home in silence, the Doctor having lapsed into brooding introspection, Martha aware of the pain in her hands and arms. Actually, now she came to think of it, her inner ear was throbbing again, as predicted by the research station's machines. She felt rather dejected and sorry for herself as she slumped on some cushions in the main living area of Petr and Kristine's house.

Kristine must have picked up her feelings as, within minutes of Martha's return, Petr's wife stood in the doorway, somewhat nervously, with a small, steaming bowl of liquid in her hands.

'Hello,' said Martha, forcing a brightness of tone into her voice that she did not feel.

'You've hurt yourself,' said Kristine simply. 'Saul told me.' Kristine bent down, the bowl still in her hands, and for a moment Martha thought she was expected to drink the strange, swirling fluid. Instead, Kristine took out what looked like long, supple slivers of bark, and used these to dab the liquid onto the scratches on Martha's hands. Martha felt a strange heat spreading into the cuts – it wasn't unpleasant, and reminded Martha of unexpected sunlight on a crisp winter's day. Within moments the pain was gone. The scratches were still visible, but already the skin seemed to be closing together to seal the wounds.

'Wow,' said Martha. 'That stuff really works!'

Kristine smiled her usual demure smile, though she seemed puzzled by Martha's surprise.

'I feel fine,' said Martha. 'Even my ear's better now!' She thought of her years of medical training, and the difficulty conventional therapies sometimes had in dealing with even relatively minor problems. And yet here Kristine was, able to administer aid easily and swiftly.

The Doctor bent down to look – Martha hadn't heard him come into the room. 'I'm still gobsmacked,' he admitted. 'The things we can do in this world, the effect it can have on us…'

'The pain seems real enough,' said Martha, still staring at her hands.

'Yeah,' said the Doctor. 'That's what worries me…'

The Doctor and Martha followed Kristine into the kitchen. They watched Saul, Petr and Kristine move silently around the room. Despite the lack of space, there seemed to be a distance between them all, even if the 'banquet' they were preparing was intended to draw the two brothers together. Doubtless their disagreements about exploring further into the forest had come to a head when Petr and Kristine's son had disappeared; the grief and mourning had in turn forced a wedge between Petr and his wife. Petr seemed to be a diligent leader, well used to tackling other people's problems and working for the good of the entire community. Now he was trying to mend a rift within his own family, and the extra weight that this put on his shoulders seemed almost too much to bear.

Martha watched Petr and the others as they chopped vegetables and skinned rabbits. The three barely spoke – the house was silent but for the crackle of the fire and the noise of blade on chopping board – and the Doctor was forced to lean towards Martha so that he could whisper in her ear.

'We've got to get out of here,' he said, an unusual urgency in his voice. 'We've got to get back to the *Castor*.'

'Why the rush? You were the one who wanted to explore.' She glanced around, her own voice becoming a whisper.

The Doctor paused for a moment before continuing. 'We think this place... snapped into existence this morning while we were exploring the station, right?'

'Well, yeah,' said Martha. 'I suppose.'

'I didn't tell you earlier,' said the Doctor. 'When I scanned Saul... some of his readings were of a perfectly normal thirty-five-year-old bloke. And some said he was only four hours old!'

'What?'

'So, for sake of argument, let's assume that all this is some sort of vast computer simulation, some... imagined world for the benefit of the people that live here.'

'I thought you said you *didn't* think it was virtual reality,' said Martha.

'Just bear with me,' said the Doctor, impatient. 'What if the land and the people are one? What if when all the people go to sleep... Everything else switches off?'

'So you're saying this whole world stops when everyone falls asleep?'

'Why not?' said the Doctor. 'Something the Dazai said earlier – when we sleep, if we're not dreaming... It's as if the universe blinks out of existence.'

'And what's this got to do with us?'

'We don't belong here,' said the Doctor. 'We can interact with this environment, but we're not sustained by it. We breath its air, we can feel the soil under our feet – we can be hurt by its inhabitants. But if I'm right and the *Castor* switches back to night-time mode to save energy... And whatever is maintaining this world just turns it off until morning...'

'Surely we'd find ourselves back on the research station,' said Martha.

The Doctor sighed. 'It might not be as simple as that. We've walked for *miles*. For all I know we're actually in deep space now, with just this bubble of unreality protecting us from…'

Martha swallowed hard, imagining the vast and deadly emptiness of space. Suddenly the ground she stood on felt a lot less solid. Without thinking she gripped the Doctor's arm for support.

'What are we going to do?' she asked.

'Get back into the forest,' said the Doctor. 'We've got to find the point where we appeared – the metal floor, the tree with the impression of a door on it. That's our best chance.'

'Saul says the woods are full of monsters that stop you going too far,' said Martha.

'Then he'd best be our guide,' said the Doctor. 'Hopefully he can take us back to the clearing where he found us.'

Martha nodded. She supposed it made sense. 'If what you're saying is true… It explains something weird that happened earlier.'

'Oh?'

'When Saul and I came back from the forest…' Martha thought for a moment, trying to remember where she had seen the sun setting. 'We appeared on the north side of the village, over by the lake.'

'But when you left…'

'We left the village heading south, towards the woods.' She paused. 'There's no way we can have looped around like that. Absolutely no way. What we did was… impossible.'

'Space is folded up on itself,' observed the Doctor. 'You can probably walk in a straight line and find yourself back where you began.'

'But why's this happening?'

'To conserve energy, I suppose,' said the Doctor. 'Just like the day/night cycle on the *Castor*. This world… It's not running off a couple of triple-A batteries, you know. When I was inspecting the Dazai's library, the books seemed normal enough at first. Loads of information, vast amounts of data, all written down in ink, page after page… And then suddenly the books became blank…'

'Like you'd used up all the data in a computer's memory or something?' said Martha. 'There's a delay as new data has to be fetched from somewhere else.'

The Doctor nodded. 'And remember how it felt like we were going round in circles in the forest? Well, perhaps we were.'

'We couldn't go any further until the next bit of reality was ready for us,' said Martha.

'Yeah, that's right.'

Martha considered this for a few moments. 'Reminds me a bit of when you're dreaming,' said Martha. 'Your mind only supplies the important bits of information, and pretty much makes the rest of it up as you go along. Even changing the rules if it has to, like you'll start off somewhere, then imagine you're somewhere else, but with some important feature of the first location carried over…'

'That's exactly it,' said the Doctor. 'But whose dream is this? And can we get out of it again?'

'You think all this is some sort of dream?' asked Martha.

'Whatever it is,' said the Doctor, 'it seems to be breaking down. Those children that are going missing – it's like having a broken hard drive in a computer. Random chunks of data are just being lost.'

'But these are people!' exclaimed Martha. 'They're not just strings of zeros and ones!'

'Are they?' said the Doctor. 'They look like people, behave like people – I'll grant you that…'

'But you're always the one telling me not to jump to conclusions,' said Martha. 'What right have we to assume that these people don't really exist? Whatever they are – they're people, they matter, they have consciousness!'

She paused for a moment, almost physically shaking, wondering where all that had come from, wondering what the Doctor would say. She was also aware that Petr, Saul and Kristine had paused momentarily and were now looking at her intently.

The Doctor waited for the others – who said nothing in response to Martha's outburst – to return to their chores before continuing. 'Of course,' he said in a quiet voice, 'you're absolutely right.' He sounded determined – and calm. 'We will bring the children back. We can do that from the space station.'

He turned back to Martha, his face strongly lined by shadow. 'But I don't think either of us want to be standing right here when reality itself boils away, do you?'

EIGHT

Jude was a good girl and always did what her mother told her. Or, rather, on those occasions when she *didn't* do what she was told, Jude always made certain the benefit was worth the risk, and then ensured that her mother never found out.

Jude lay in bed, looking at the stars through the window. She had opened the shutters once her mother had gone back downstairs – the creaking board four steps from the bottom meant Jude always knew when someone had moved out of earshot.

It was a perfect night, with barely a cloud in the sky – though, if she propped herself up on her elbows, she could see that the fog was seeping out of the woods and across the lake towards the village. She kept glimpsing shapes moving about in the mist, then sternly told herself that if you look at *anything* expecting to see *something*, you'll find it soon enough. The reality was,

Jude was hoping to see Farah again, though whether this was out of fear or expectation, Jude wasn't quite sure.

Her mother had said that Saul was going for a meal with Uncle Petr and Auntie Kristine, but that her father was going on his own because he had 'bridges to mend'. Jude wished grown-ups wouldn't keep covering over reality with flowery language – it was obvious to everyone that Saul and Petr just liked arguing with each other. The sad truth of the matter was that sometimes Saul became angry, and he didn't want his daughter or wife around if the two men came to blows.

Jude had asked her mother if the two strangers would be there as well, and she'd said that she supposed so, given that they were honoured guests and were staying with Petr and Kristine. Jude had then asked if the Dazai would be joining them, and her mother had replied that Petr was wary of the old woman and her cryptic advice – and so should Jude be, if she had any sense. Jude hadn't, in actual fact, seen much of the Dazai over the years, preferring impersonal books from the library to the Dazai's rambling and elusive wisdom. Anyway, the Dazai seemed to have far too many teeth missing. *And* she smelled funny – she stank of old skin and hair, not like the wonderful, musky aroma of the documents and manuscripts Jude loved to pore over.

Jude slipped out of bed and started pulling on her thickest blue robes. A pillow under the sheets should fool anyone who glanced in, though she only planned to be gone an hour or so at most. There was something important going on within the village, something that impacted on the future of everyone who lived there, and yet most people seemed to want to ignore it. Not Jude – her aim was to be there when important things happened and, just at the moment, that meant being close to the Doctor and his friend. For all his silly words and occasional moments of unsettling mania, the Doctor had 'importance' stamped all over him.

The window creaked open, and Jude held her breath for a moment – but no one was coming up the stairs. Indeed, it sounded as if her mother was still moving about in the kitchen, tidying away the remains of the small meal they had shared together while father spoke in low tones about the rabbits he'd got for the feast at Petr's house.

There was a great, knotted vine growing up at the back of the house. It pushed its tendrils into wood and slate and stone and now appeared almost part of the structure, though these days it rarely managed to sprout any glossy orange leaves. Perhaps this was because Jude used it so often for escape – anyone looking closely at the ground beneath her bedroom window would have seen stripped bark and a scattering of frayed leaves.

But no one looked at the back of Jude's home, because no one knew that Jude ever escaped this way.

Jude lowered herself out of the window – each bend and swelling of the vine absolutely familiar to her – and began to descend towards the ground, pushing the window shut behind her. She wished sometimes her father had built a smaller house – most of the buildings in the village were simple, single-storey dwellings, but her father had always said that his traps and hunting equipment required a lot of space. Indeed, there were rooms that Jude had never even glanced into, though she imagined them piled from floor to ceiling with trophies of his prowess. Stuffed and mounted heads of bears and wolves, no doubt – and maybe even the remains of the monsters that he sometimes talked about when he'd had a drop of ale. Jude's mother always told Saul to be quiet at those moments, and he'd refuse to elaborate when Jude questioned him later, so the beasts in the outermost forest had for a long time lived only in Jude's mind, as great monsters in the darkness and mementoes in mysterious, locked chambers. Now, of course, she knew them to be real – the Doctor's friend Martha had seen them. Worse still, she'd said they were coming closer to the village.

Jude stepped down onto the ground and began to walk towards the green at the heart of the village, hugging the shadows and the edges of the houses. Once or twice, she was passed by men talking in low tones – patrols or just fathers returning home after an evening in the inn, she wasn't quite sure – but she simply stopped each time and pressed further back into the darkness, and they moved on soon enough.

From the green she skirted around the bakery – it smelt luxuriously of wheat and yeast even when the ovens were cool, as they were now – and then ducked into a small, ornate garden of cultivated plants and hanging lanterns. Moments later she was outside her uncle's impressive home. Light poured from the dining room window. It always reminded her of the great feasting chamber at the heart of the village hall, though in truth it was a good deal smaller. Whereas the whole village came together in the great hall to commemorate the passing of the seasons and successful harvests, Petr and Kristine's dining room was often used for family events – an obscure uncle's first child, a cousin's unexpected marriage. Jude couldn't help but wonder how much longer it would be before Petr and Kristine accepted the inevitable and marked the loss of their son.

Hearing voices, Jude crept under the window. Everyone was talking – it sounded like her father had been drinking a little and was louder than usual, making some bad joke at Petr's expense – and the Doctor and his friend Martha were using this as the backdrop to another one of their whispered conversations.

'You said you'd tell me why the name of this place was important,' said Martha.

'Just a vague echo in the name of this place, that's all,' said the Doctor. '*Herot*. Battle-hall in an old poem. I wasn't sure it meant much at first, but now…' Jude caught a sigh from the traveller. 'It's as if so much of

Earth culture has been boiled down and presented to us as a living, breathing reality. And just think of the people we've met – the brave hunter, the thoughtful leader, the wise old woman...'

Safely hidden in the shadows, Jude scratched her head. She couldn't follow half of what was said, but the tone was clear enough – both the Doctor and Martha were tense, as if finalising a secret plan. Both seemed impatient to leave, though the Doctor was better at hiding his concerns.

'You mean they're... archetypes?' said Martha, moments later.

'That's how they seem to have started,' said the Doctor. 'But, you're right, now they've changed, developed, evolved...'

'With monsters pressing in on them, and legends about dead children rising from a lake,' added Martha. 'And it's night-time. So in a few hours everyone in the village will be asleep, the research station will switch to its night cycle...'

'And if we're still here it'll be *Hello, vacuum; hello, deep space*...'

There was a pause, footsteps from within the room – instinctively Jude pressed herself even further into the shadows under the window. She glanced around. The fog was thicker than ever now and the shapes within it, the patterns of movement, were getting more pronounced all the time.

'Have you enjoyed your meal?' Petr's voice sounded incredibly close to Jude. He must have been standing at the window, half-turned to the Doctor and his friend.

'It was lovely!' exclaimed the Doctor. 'My compliments to your dear wife.'

'She is a woman of many talents,' said Petr in a low voice. 'I am lucky to have her.'

Underneath the window, Jude resisted the temptation to make gagging noises.

'I'm afraid we must be going,' said Martha.

'So soon?'

'I'm sorry, Petr. You've been very hospitable, but... We're needed elsewhere.'

'You won't stay the night?' persisted Petr.

'Impossible, I'm afraid,' said the Doctor firmly. 'We'll come back tomorrow, but for the moment...'

'You have been an ambassador like no other,' admitted Petr. 'I'm still not sure of your purpose amongst us,' he said with a chuckle.

Before the Doctor could say anything, Jude heard the dining room door slide open with a crash. Petr's laughter died away to nothing as someone rushed into the room, sobbing and incoherent. An awful hush fell over the room, punctuated by cries and the sound of Auntie Kristine trying to comfort the newcomer.

Another set of footsteps across the oak floorboards brought Jude's father towards the Doctor, Martha and Petr.

'Another disappearance,' said Saul simply. 'The Sabato family.'

As the wailing within Petr's house increased in pitch, Jude turned once more to the fog that drifted and surged through the village. She imagined, just for a moment, that she could see a new figure in there – a new child now one with the fog.

The Doctor and Martha ran, at once, to the household that had been overcome by tragedy, but there was – literally – nothing to see. The child's window was locked from the inside, and the bedroom door led straight into the family's living quarters, where mother and father had sat all evening, staring at the dying embers of the fire in the grate. The child's bed was still warm, and the mother found a single strand of golden hair upon the pillow. Her face crumpled and, despite her husband's stoic presence, the wailing began once more.

The Doctor turned to Petr, his face both uncomprehending and defiant. 'We'll sort this out,' he said firmly. 'I promise. But we've got to go back into the forest. We must go back to the spot where Saul found us.'

'Now?'

'Yes, now.'

Petr had turned to his brother, who was standing at his side and trying to calm the hysterical mother of the disappeared child. 'You will take them, of course?' It was part question, part statement.

Saul nodded curtly. 'I will.' He paused for a moment, still looking at his brother. 'You will come with us…?'

Petr shook his head. 'No. My business is here, in the village – with those who suffer loss and hardship. The woods are your territory.'

'Within *your* parameters,' Saul muttered under his breath.

'Sorry?'

'I thought the Doctor and Martha were your guests,' said Saul, more loudly. 'I thought…'

'Yes?'

Saul turned to the Doctor and Martha. 'I thought you would help us.'

'We will,' said the Doctor. 'But we need to leave the village. Once we're away from here I'll be in a better position to help you.'

Saul turned away without saying anything else – Martha couldn't tell if he took the Doctor's words at face value or if he was disappointed by what he'd heard.

Petr smiled with official finality. 'It is arranged then,' he said.

And so it was, with seemingly indecent haste, that Martha and the Doctor found themselves once more back in the forest. They both carried a sputtering torch, though Saul preferred to have his hands free. Martha thought at first this was to enable him to push aside the toughest branches without encumbrance, but then she noticed the swords at his belt. He carried two this time, though in truth one was barely longer than a dagger. But just before they'd left she'd glanced out of the window and seen Saul polishing his blades and carefully sheathing them. Saul was, if anything, even more on edge than normal.

'It's not far,' he breathed after some time, dropping to his knees to examine tracks on the ground. 'This used to be a safe place,' he added sadly, 'but with the creatures gaining ground all the time…'

'Does that belong to one of the monsters?' asked Martha, pointing at the tracks.

Saul shook his head. 'Bears,' he said. 'Though, if they've been disturbed by what's been going on… You still wouldn't want to run into one of them.'

Martha didn't especially want to run into a bear, whatever its mood.

They trudged along for some considerable time, Martha desperate to spot something she recognised from their first appearance in the woods that morning. But it was dark now, the trees reaching around and over her like suffocating shadows, and it was all she could do to keep her feet from stumbling over hidden roots and broken branches. She'd have to trust in Saul.

'We're almost there,' said Saul suddenly as they came into a clearing. The harsh lines of the trees were dappled and softened by starlight.

'Yes!' exclaimed Martha suddenly, pointing to a small

stump a distance away. It resembled a squashed teddy bear. 'I remember this bit….'

'I found you just over there,' said Saul, pointing, 'and you were coming from this direction.' And he set off again.

Martha turned to the Doctor. 'Is it much further?'

'Hard to tell in this place,' said the Doctor. 'We were going around in circles when we first arrived. Perhaps, with Saul's help—'

The silence of the dark forest was suddenly split asunder. Someone was screaming at the top of their voice – a shrill, instinctive noise. A child.

'Come on!' said the Doctor, already at Saul's shoulder and running at his side.

Within moments they found themselves in another small open space between the trees. The floor of the clearing was covered with moss and tiny brambles, and in the centre crouched a girl in pale blue robes.

'Jude!' exclaimed Saul, running forward with blind fatherly concern. 'What are you doing out here?'

The girl struggled against Saul's embrace, pointing in wordless terror as a vast creature pushed its way into the clearing. It moved with surprising grace for all its bulk, hugging close to the ground.

Martha gulped – it was the creature they had glimpsed when Saul had freed the Doctor from the iron trap. If you put a dragon and a spider in a blender, she decided, and then gave the result to Dracula as a pet… *That* would be the result. It had an emaciated, lizard-like face and body, and huge bat wings, though the skin between the bones was tattered and grey. Its legs tapped against the ground when it paused, as if it were feeling its way towards its prey. Arched above its head was a great spiked tail.

Before anyone could shout a warning the tail came smashing downwards, right into the centre of the clearing where Saul and Jude sat. Saul moved his daughter to one side and himself to the other, just as the bony spikes thudded into the decayed tree trunks beneath them. The rotting wood shattered, sending splinters high into the air – but at least the two were safe.

Jude went running immediately towards the Doctor and Martha, but Saul stood his ground. A sword in each hand now, he crossed the blades in front of his face, as if daring the beast to come closer.

He twisted his head to one side. 'Look after Jude.'

The tail came down again, glancing off an upright tree. In any event, Saul was taking no chances, leaping into the air like a gymnast, then running through two of the creature's legs. He arced his swords upwards as he ran. Both bit deep into the creature's flesh. Then he positioned himself behind the creature, where he could not be seen.

'Run!' he shouted, risking a great cut to the creature's rump while avoiding its feverishly flailing tail. The monster was swinging round in an attempt to bring its great, snapping jaws into play, its attention entirely focused on Saul.

'Come on!' breathed the Doctor, holding Jude's arm and almost pushing Martha out of the clearing. 'I think it's this way!'

'Daddy!' shrieked Jude.

'He'll be all right,' said the Doctor. 'Promise!'

'We can't just leave him!' shouted Martha, half-turning.

'Of course we're not going to leave him!' exclaimed the Doctor. They were some metres beyond the clearing now, and he stopped suddenly. Facing the many-legged creature, he pulled the sonic screwdriver from his pocket, adjusted the settings with nimble fingers, and then held it high in the air.

The end of the screwdriver glowed brightly and Martha heard a shrill whine, which ascended in pitch and soon became completely inaudible – but a moment later its effect on the monster was all too clear to see.

It ceased its attack on Saul, its scaly head turning towards the Doctor.

'Doggy whistle!' he announced proudly, still holding the sonic screwdriver over his head.

'Can't you kill it?' asked Martha.

'Why should I want to do that?' asked the Doctor. 'Hasn't done anything to hurt us...'

'Yet.'

'When I say "run"...' the Doctor breathed as the

monster scuttled towards them on its spine-covered legs.

He turned, to find himself on his own. Martha and Jude were thundering down a natural path between the trees.

'Oh,' he said. 'Right.'

He sprinted away, still gripping the screwdriver tightly. The beast announced its departure from the clearing by swiping down as many trees as it could. From Saul's shouts and curses, it seemed that the hunter was, in turn, pursuing the creature – and he didn't much approve of the Doctor's bravery.

'You'll thank me later, Saul,' said the Doctor, under his breath. Behind him, the dragon seemed to be getting closer all the time. Though the creature remained stoically silent, the Doctor could hear the flap of its wings, the hiss of its tail through the air – and the sound of still more trees being smashed to the ground. Each noise was getting louder, like a grim orchestra swelling to a finale.

He risked a glance over his shoulder – just as the monster's tail flew through the air like a wrecking ball against a derelict building.

The Doctor threw himself to one side, then jumped the opposite way – another *thud!* as the spikes impacted only against tree and soil – all the while running as fast as he could after the fleeing figures of Martha and Jude.

'Not far now,' he said, probably for the umpteenth

time that day. 'Just hope we get there in one piece!'

Even over the noise of the pursuing creature, even over the fevered survival instinct that was threatening to swamp all her senses, Martha tried to keep a clear head and work out where she was going. She forced herself to look at the trees and bushes as they disappeared past her in a blur of grey shadow. She knew there was no point just running aimlessly through the trees – they had to find the clearing that seemed to lead back to the research station.

Jude ran feverishly at her side, whimpering under her breath – in terror, or in fear for her father, Martha couldn't tell which – but not once did she fall or stumble or put a foot wrong.

'This is it!' exclaimed Martha, skidding to a halt and almost falling to her knees. 'Look!' She jogged forward, pointed to the tree that bore the faintest of impressions of a hard metal door. Jude simply stared, uncomprehending and silent.

The Doctor, sonic screwdriver between his teeth, thundered into the clearing, knocking Martha over. 'Turned it off,' he said, dropping the screwdriver into a pocket and helping Martha to her feet. 'Doesn't seem to have made any difference,' he added pointlessly, as the noise of trees being torn asunder made it quite clear that the dragon-thing was almost upon them. 'Seem to have over-egged the pudding a touch,' he added, with a grin.

Martha pointed at the tree with the shadow of the door seemingly stamped onto its trunk. 'There,' she said, still panting.

The Doctor brandished the sonic screwdriver, waving it in front of the tree and changing its settings all the time.

The creature edged into the clearing, but its back was towards them now. It looked like Saul had started to irritate it once again, dancing in front of the monster like a frantic, diminutive manikin, shouting and slashing when the opportunity arose.

'Dad!' exclaimed Jude, about to run towards her father, but Martha held her tight.

'Hurry!' Martha hissed at the Doctor, then tried to soothe the struggling child. 'It's OK, we're *all* going to get out of here…'

Suddenly the very trees around them began to flicker. Like two random images pasted one on top of the other, Martha glimpsed the enclosed, almost featureless corridor of the space research station *Castor* stretching into the distance beside her. The Doctor seemed to be succeeding in overlaying the reality of the spaceship over the illusion of the forest. But then the vast and forested vista returned, apparently even more solid, even more real, than the glimpsed metal corridor.

'Almost there!' shouted the Doctor, still adjusting the screwdriver.

Martha glanced down at Jude, who paused in her

struggles. Martha wondered if the collision between twin realities was only visible to her and the Doctor, or if the girl could see the space station too.

The dragon-beast, however, seemed momentarily disturbed, pausing in its attack. It swung its head from side to side, distracted.

Martha turned to the Doctor – just as Jude wriggled free and shot across the forest clearing towards her father – in the direction of the metal corridor that had been visible a few moments before. 'No! Come back!' cried Martha, but it was too late.

And then the forest disappeared, entirely replaced by the space station corridor – and the huge airlock-style door that Martha remembered coming through to get into the forest in the first place. Of the beast, of Jude and Saul, there was suddenly no sign. They had faded with the forest.

It was utterly silent, and the Doctor and Martha were absolutely alone on the space station.

'Where did they go?' asked Martha.

'Still in the forest,' said the Doctor quickly. 'It's here, all around us, in another part of reality – a world all of its own which we can't see any more.' He pointed the sonic screwdriver at the huge door, and the screwdriver emitted an ear-shredding whine. 'But the forest world might reassert itself at any time, and then we will be trapped inside it again. We've got to get this door open. We'll be safe on the other side. The space station is stable through there – the forest doesn't reach beyond this door.'

'What about Saul and Jude?'

'They are exactly where they were – where we used to be. We can help them from here! Trust me. If you stay and the forest world comes back, you might die!'

'I might not!'

The door began to roll open, showing another bland stretch of corridor beyond. Safety, away from the possibility of encroaching forest. But then the walls around Martha began to flicker again – the trees coming back into view all around them. Only the area beyond the door was clear and safe. Looking back, Martha could see the creature on the far side of the clearing, but Saul seemed to have fallen to the ground. For the first time, the beast was making a triumphant, hissing sound – its huge mouth stretched open, its spiked tail ready to strike.

Of Jude there was absolutely no sign.

'Doctor, we've got to help them!'

The Doctor had fully opened the door now and was stepping through. He reached out a hand to encourage Martha to follow him. 'Everything you see could cease to exist at any moment,' he observed. 'But you've got to go through this door to where it's safe. I can't keep the link between the worlds open much longer!'

Martha looked at the Doctor, then stared back at Saul, crumpled before the might of the squealing beast.

Around her, the corridor kept slamming into focus, and then blinking away again. Corridor. Forest. Corridor. Forest.

The dragon swung its tail up over its head one last time.

'Sorry!' she breathed, letting go of the Doctor's hand and running as fast as she could towards Saul.

If the Doctor made a sound, she could not hear it over the noise of the door grinding shut. She glanced back, over her shoulder – the space station had entirely vanished, leaving only the faintest imprint on the trees and ground around her.

She was back in the forest. She was on her own.

And the creature was about to kill Saul.

NINE

Jens rolled uncertainly out of the inn, torch in hand. In the last hour, the fog had thickened and clotted until it gripped the edge of every building and pathway, dulling them and replacing familiar lines and spaces with subtle gradations of grey. Even more alarming was the change in temperature. It had seemed quite mild when Jens had staggered into the warm, embracing bosom of the inn – he'd left his scarf and his thickest cloak at home, partly because he was sure he'd not need them, and partly because speed had been of the essence and he'd wanted to get away as quickly as possible. But now the air was as keen as a shard of ice.

Jens shivered, fumbling at the torch with his great, gloved hands, while a voice nagged in his mind. *I told you it was going to turn cold, but did you listen? No, nothing must come between the big man and his drink – not storm, not cold, not common sense! I sometimes wonder why I put up with you,*

Jens, really I do…

He paused, wondering for a moment if there was time to duck back into the inn and order one last flagon, but shuffled footsteps and scraped chairs from within indicated that Shih and her diminutive husband had decided to call it a night. Torch now sullenly lit, Jens started to walk away; he did not turn and bid the others farewell, nor did they call good wishes after him. Almost all had sat within the inn simply to escape from the outside world; none of them now seemed pleased to be returning to it.

Soon Jens was on his own, treading familiar streets in fogged silence. The alcohol sat heavy in his stomach, and he struggled desperately to control his runaway thoughts; it was ironic, he supposed, that he drank to forget, and all it did was make the memories and the guilt ever stronger. 'Why don't you come back?' he found himself whispering – or maybe he was shouting like a drunkard and the sound was simply muffled by the fog.

Cursing his own stupidity, he paused for a moment, breathing heavily. He'd have to creep in discreetly, not crash through his home like a fat skittle knocked aside by a ball. 'Shh,' he told himself. 'Nice and easy does it.'

He looked around – he was close to the metalsmith's workshop, its precise walls studded with windows and flaps that helped the big, brutish fellow keep the furnace at just the right temperature. But there was no illumination within the place now, and precious few other lanterns or discernible objects to help Jens work out where he was. Moments later, he paused, scratching his head – had he gone too far? It was hard to be sure, the fog seeming to dull his senses as much as his vision. Should he double back and make sure he turned left at the marble fountain that overlooked the green?

Before Jens could decide, a tiny, delicate noise began to wrap itself around the cotton-wool silence. The noise grew louder, but never became shrill or overbearing. It seemed indistinguishable from the mist and the darkness, coming from every direction at once – and nowhere.

It was a girl, singing.

Where the water flows round and round
The crooked tree that we found –
Where I found you and you found me,
And brothers, sisters, find not one of three –
We shall meet there and tread soft,
And let hat and coat and shoe be doffed,
Lest bird and animal hear our call
And one by one, unpitied, fall.

It was a childish rhyme, of course, an almost tuneless play on words that Jens remembered his mother singing to him when he couldn't sleep. She used to embellish and add words and fall over herself in a desperate attempt to follow the rhythm of the thing. Jens in turn had sung it to…

'Shiga?'

He turned on the spot, desperate to hear the voice again, desperate to discover another reason to hope, to imagine, to *believe*...

'Is that you, girl?' he called out into the unreal silence – it was as if he stood alone in a void, with nothing around him but a bank of fog, and a memory – or an echo – of the girl's voice.

'Shiga?' he called out, more loudly this time, but no reply came back to him.

Jens shook his head and, cursing the ale he'd had, he started to stumble back towards his house – though unsure of the direction now, he was sure he'd soon see something he recognised.

Without warning the ethereal singing began again.

Where the water flows round and round
The crooked tree that we found –
Where I found you and you found me,
And brothers, sisters, find not one of three...

A tiny, drained, grey figure stepped from the shadows and into the sputtering light of the torch. Hair that was once burned like ripe cornfields fell about the child's shoulders like silver chains; eyes and cheeks that had been bright with life were as pale as the enveloping mist.

But the features, the voice that chimed like tiny bells – they were unmistakeable.

'Shiga!' Without thinking, Jens took a step forward

– and the girl sank back into the fog, as if keeping her distance. She resolutely finished her song, her voice cracking with emotion.

We shall meet there and tread soft,
And let hat and coat and shoe be doffed,
Lest bird and animal hear our call
And one by one, unpitied, fall…

A single tear tracked a serpentine line down her cheek.

'Father,' she said formally, half-bowing in the breath between words, 'why did you let me fall?'

'My love, I would never…'

She interrupted him, a sound like gathered wind. 'You let me fall! You let me down, day by day, and you were too fond of drink to see it!'

'No, my love… I only started drinking when you… When you left.'

'You were drinking long before that!' The girl's eyes were pearls no longer, but dark, compressed stone. 'I lost you years ago – and only recently have you lost me…'

Jens paused, deep in thought. Had it really been like that? Was she right – had the long nights in the inn, staring into a muddled succession of tankards and glasses, started *before* she had been snatched away in the fog?

'I'm sorry,' he said, the words tumbling without thought or pretence. 'I'm so sorry…' And his own tears fell now, burning against his skin.

The girl seemed unsure of herself, as if, of all possible reactions, this was the one she had least expected. 'Father,' she said, in a voice as quiet as an infant's sigh. 'Dad…'

'Yes, my love?' Jens looked up, though he could hardly bear to look at her – she seemed so pale, so fragile, he feared she would fade away before his eyes.

'Know this!' she suddenly exclaimed, her lips pulled back, her face tight to her skull like a death mask. 'The children shall return – and we will *all* be destroyed!'

And she swept over and through him like a dark angel, and Jens stumbled, then ran, into the grey heart of the fog. His screams and cries were soon swallowed up, and silence gripped the village once more.

Emerging from a void of sleep and shadow, Jude became aware of something hard and unyielding under her back, and something damp on one side of her face.

She struggled into a seated position, holding herself tight, trying to stop her teeth chattering. She was in some sort of building – the ground beneath her was as smooth and as flat as wood, but felt like iron or steel – and it was almost completely dark. And the moisture she felt on her skin was a small patch of blood, just beginning to thicken and clot.

She wasn't in the forest any more.

Her last memory was of tugging herself free of Martha and running towards her father. Something strange was happening – she kept glimpsing a single silver corridor, and she wondered if she was nearly dying and this was the way to heaven. But she wasn't injured, she didn't feel unwell – and the monster was attacking her father. Compared to that awful reality, nothing else mattered.

She had darted towards him, screaming his name, oblivious to the great creature, its wings stretched out as if to cover the sky. Suddenly, everything around her changed, a new reality crashing over the old one. She was in darkness, in some sort of echoing chamber – and she was falling.

She must have hit the floor and passed out. Now she stood, trying desperately to see shapes in the darkness. Her ears strained for any sound, but they throbbed only with silence. Of her father, of the monster, of the forest, there seemed to be no trace.

Swallowing down her panic, she started to explore her enclosed environment, her feet echoing against the floor. Definitely metal of some sort. She was indoors, somewhere. And everything was very, very dark.

She walked for a few moments, hands outstretched before her. She told herself not to be scared – she wasn't a baby, she knew that she wasn't *necessarily* in danger just because she couldn't see where she was going – but, even so, the sooner she found a lantern or a window, the better.

She took a few more steps and found a wall, hewn seemingly from the same strong, resilient metal as the floor. She pushed herself on tiptoes, stretched her arms in either direction as far as she could – nothing. The wall seemed entirely featureless and smooth.

She edged along it, still feeling her way with outstretched arms and cautious, shuffling footsteps. Suddenly she stumbled into something, about waist-height and very solid. She ran her hands across it nervously, but it seemed to be just a box, absolutely square and seemingly made of some sort of faintly warm, plant-like material. There was no obvious lid to the box, nothing else to indicate its purpose or to give her reason to examine it further. She groped further into the gloom, forcing herself to breathe slowly, batting away each fear as it came to mind. *What if I don't get out? What if I'm imprisoned forever? How can I get back to the forest? What's happened to Dad?*

'Shh,' she hissed, irritated at herself. 'Let's just find a door.'

The moment she spoke, a dim light began to seep into the room. She nervously dropped to her knees, seeking shelter behind another one of the plain boxes. 'Who's there?' she asked, but there was no reply. However, the light grew a little stronger, painting everything with a dull yellow colour.

She looked around her – the room was smaller than she had thought, not much larger than her bedroom, though the ceiling was high. The light came from the ceiling; a series of lanterns, about the size of small vanity mirrors, were built into the roof. The ceiling and the walls seemed utterly featureless. Thankfully, one of the walls was studded with a simple, rectangular door – the edges where door met wall, and what looked like hinges, were just visible. And scattered across the floor were a number of mostly square buff-coloured brown boxes. Each one was sealed, and strange hieroglyphs had been written or stamped across their sides. Some were piled high and pushed back into the corner of the room, others seemed scattered almost randomly.

She walked towards the door, but her inquisitive mind refused to let things rest there. Why had the lights come on? They didn't seem like windows, so where was the light coming from?

'Hello!' she said suddenly, her tiny voice now sounding brash and loud as it echoed and rebounded off the metal walls. Obediently, the lights in the ceiling became yet more dazzling. It was like daylight, somehow captured in a room without windows.

Jude stepped up to the door, wondering how she was going to open it – she could see no lock, no handle, and she imagined it was as at least as thick as the walls and floor.

Suddenly the door opened. It slid noiselessly back into the wall, rather like the interior doors of Jude's house, but it appeared to complete the action on its own. The shock and sudden movement was so great that Jude immediately jumped backwards.

Unbidden, the door emerged from its slot between the walls, gliding into place and clicking shut again. For the first time, Jude could hear a faint humming sound coming from the door.

Jude took a couple of deep breaths and walked forward once more.

The door immediately slid away. Jude scratched her head, puzzled. There was no one there, but the door seemed entirely capable of moving on its own.

She stepped out onto the corridor beyond – it was silver-coloured and, like the room, was very plain. It was incredibly long, stretching off in both directions – this house must be huge, she thought, the palace of some great king. The style reminded her of what she had seen in the forest. The place she had glimpsed while her father fought the dragon-creature was now her reality, and the forest might as well have been a dream.

She paused, forcing back the tide of panic that threatened to drown her, and wondered which way to turn. She could hear and smell nothing from either direction, and both corridors appeared identical.

Shrugging her shoulders, she turned left out of the cell and crept along the floor, keeping low as she had seen her father do on numerous occasions. She passed another door – which also opened as she approached – but the room beyond only contained more boxes, and no one answered her when she called out.

The corridor turned abruptly to the right. As she

followed it she stopped suddenly – and shivered.

One section of the corridor was as black as midnight. The lights over her head became progressively dim until, at the far end, there was no illumination at all, and even the featureless walls flickered with shadow.

And something was moving within the darkness.

Martha ran forward, giving in to instinct and the urge to try to save Saul. 'Oi!' she shouted. 'Pick on someone your own size!' she added moments later – not the most original thing she'd ever said, but she didn't suppose the creature would notice.

The creature quickly snapped its head to one side to examine Martha, a pair of its legs still resting on Saul's motionless chest. Martha supposed it was like a cat playing with its – still living – food. Now Martha was providing another, equally tempting target. It hissed once, then sprang forward nimbly, wings folded flat against its body. Like an industrial piston, its face came forward – all teeth and spittle and the stench of rotting meat – and Martha ducked out of the way. Then she jumped, narrowly avoiding the great, sweeping tail that was aimed at her legs.

Next a huge leg thudded into the undergrowth like an arrow fired by some grim giant – she felt it rather than saw it and pitched backwards into some bushes – followed by another, and another. Martha rolled to her left – then right – then pushed herself onto her hands and knees. The beast towered above her. Its wings, unfurled against the night sky, cut the moon in two.

Another needle-tipped leg swung down; Martha swayed away from it like a boxer, but it was only a trick to divert her attention. The tail – as thick as a tree trunk – flew over the forest floor and into her legs, knocking her onto her back. Her view of the dark starscape shook violently as she crashed to the ground; for a moment she thought she was going to pass out, and then everything came back into focus.

The creature hissed triumphantly, preparing to strike. Martha screwed her eyes shut, crying out in desperation, though she knew no one was there. She cried out – and waited for the killing blow.

A second passed. Then another.

She forced open her eyes. The creature had shifted its bodyweight to one side and was now looking not at Martha, but at the apparently rejuvenated, sword-wielding man leaping through the air like an acrobat.

'Saul!' breathed Martha – but, moments later, she realised it was not the hunter. It was Petr, his angular frame lacking his brother's innate fluidity – but the great two-handed sword in his hands seemed to make up for any grace he missed. The sword came down in a near-silent arc of sharp silver against the creature's nearest, splayed leg.

It cut through fibrous skin, striated muscle and sinew, and bit finally into bone. The sword did not go too deep

– with a flick of his wrists the weapon was back over Petr's head, ready for another strike – but its effect on the creature was almost instantaneous.

Its entire body shuddered, each leg shaking in sympathy with the wounded limb, and it swung its head down and close to its body. It took two steps backwards, still staring at Petr – and hissed like a scalded cat.

Martha's eyes widened. The creature was *scared*.

'Unbelievable,' said a voice at her ear.

She turned, expecting the Doctor – but seeing only Saul. Though covered in bruises and scratches, he'd hauled himself to his feet and stood watching the creature, a wry amusement obvious on his face.

'Someone finally gets a good strike against one of these beasts,' he continued, 'and it's my brother.' He sighed. 'I may never live it down.'

And, hefting his swords upwards, and with a great cry of rage, Saul ran past his brother and towards the monster.

The Doctor knew he didn't have much time. The space station was still in its daytime mode, with each and every system operational and functioning, but there was no guarantee it would stay that way. It was surely no coincidence that Petr and Saul's world had blinked into existence soon after the lights had come on, and logic dictated it might click off just as swiftly when simulated night fell over the *Castor*. It felt like he and Martha had been away from the research ship for hours, but for the moment the Doctor had no way of verifying that.

The Doctor surmised that whatever was behind the phantom world was linked in some way to the night-and-day pattern built into the software that ran the station's systems. If it were a machine – and the technology would have to be far in advance of anything he had seen around the *Castor* – then the energy required to generate that much matter would be tremendous. There was no sign of the station generating any more energy than it needed to keep ticking over. And if there was some creature or person behind everything… Well, who dreams during the day? And what creature can possibly bring into existence a world – or a sizeable chunk of one at least – purely through the power of thought?

In fact, there were myriad questions the Doctor wanted answering – but first things first. He had to ensure the bubble world was kept going overnight – otherwise, when Petr and the others awoke the next day, they would find Martha gone, dumped unceremoniously back into the real world. And, if she was standing in just the wrong place when that happened, or if there were some other side effect of being within an unreal world when it collapsed in on itself… Well, it was quite possible the Doctor would never see her again either.

The Doctor shivered, increasing his pace, but skidded to a halt moments later in front of a computer terminal. With the help of the sonic screwdriver, and the knowledge of hardware and software systems gained over centuries and lifetimes, he hacked into the main system in minutes. Soon a complete schematic was scrolling across the screen – every room, every system, was now laid bare.

'A map!' he said out loud, reaching into his pocket for his glasses. 'You can change the world with a jolly good map!'

He stabbed impatiently at the keyboard, trying to overlay the life support details over the map, much as he had done with Martha before they'd stumbled across the forest where a corridor should have been.

'That's me,' he said, pointing at a dull blue glow standing within Technical Corridor 12, Intersection K. In other circumstances, he'd have been offended by the summary currently underneath 'his' dot – *Unknown and/ or deviant life signs detected*. But the important thing now was the range of life signs the *Castor* was picking up.

'That's the bubble world,' said the Doctor, pointing to a mass of contradictory and conflicting signals over one unimportant-looking corridor. Though seemingly condensed in material terms compared to the vast swathes of trees and mountains they had seen, the Doctor's worst fears were realised – much of the 'bubble' extended into deep space, beyond the station's hull. Hopefully – somewhere amongst that mess of signals – would be Martha's signal, still pulsing away strongly. Martha's – and the dragon-monster, of course.

'Hang on in there, Martha,' breathed the Doctor.

Elsewhere on the *Castor* there was the faintest trace of the flickering, ever-changing life form they'd noticed earlier. Once again the ship's systems were finding it hard to pin down, both biologically and temporally. Indeed, at one point, it seemed to be almost in two places at once, and then it appeared to be ascending vertically through the ship's floors and ceilings.

Even more intriguingly, there was another – fourth – signal on the screens, pulsing steadily. He hoped to goodness it was not another monster – he'd had quite enough of them for one day.

The summary underneath this fourth signal was almost as intriguing as the Doctor's – *Human, unrecognised*. The Doctor drilled down to get more information. For a split second it read *Human – female – c.12 years old – healthy – not in database*, then it flickered and became *Unknown – unknown – unknown – unknown – not in database*.

The Doctor frowned – the life support and monitoring systems were not having their best day. He tapped at the keyboard a few more times, trying to isolate where on the *Castor* the readings were coming from.

He paused momentarily, drumming his fingers against the terminal – then turned on the spot, taking his stealthy observer completely by surprise.

'Hey, Jude!' he exclaimed, delighted. 'Been wanting to say that for *ages*,' he added.

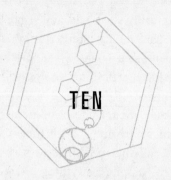

TEN

The great skeletal dragon shook its head slowly. Now that it was facing two, apparently well-armed, targets, the creature seemed to be having second thoughts. Its deep-set eyes narrowed like smouldering coals in a fire, an almost human reaction to the distress it was feeling. Two of its legs were oozing viscous blood, and both Saul and Petr had managed to slash at its wings. Its skin, which naturally seemed to fall in ragged strips from the bones, was looking even more tattered now, and the creature was making a low, moaning noise somewhere in its throat.

Emboldened, Saul ducked through the legs one more time, aiming a sword upwards at the creature's exposed flank. His sword returned to his side, stained and dripping, and he tumbled out of the way of the spiked tail as it lunged desperately towards him.

The creature shook its head one last time, folded its

wings away as neatly as it could, and began to slink back into the trees. Saul and Petr stood side by side, watching it go. 'Thank you,' said Saul quietly to his brother.

Petr nodded, saying nothing, his eyes still fixed on the retreating monster.

Martha came over, trying not to look too closely at what the men were wiping from their blades. When the two men had sheathed their swords, they turned to each other – despite everything, there was still an awkwardness between them that spoke volumes.

'We'd better get back,' said Petr abruptly.

There was a drawn-out roar from somewhere to their right – it seemed the dragon wasn't the only beast patrolling the forest. The cry sounded like it was coming from the insectoid creature Martha and Saul had encountered earlier; though currently deep in the trees, it was getting closer.

'Not until we find Jude,' said Saul firmly. His face was set and determined. He began calling out her name, his hands around his mouth to amplify his voice. His strong, desperate cries penetrated deep into the trees – and received only the bestial cry of the advancing monster in return.

'You sure shouting like that's a good idea?' queried Martha. She understood Saul's feelings for his daughter but, if they weren't careful, all they were going to do was bring every monster within a ten-kilometre radius to their position.

'She was here?' queried Petr, the colour seeming to drain from his face. He had obviously turned up too late to see his niece threatened by the creature.

Saul stopped calling, his hands now hanging limply at his side. 'She followed us,' said Saul sadly. 'Damn the impetuous child!' Despite his harsh words, his eyes were suddenly full of tears.

'She… disappeared,' said Martha carefully. 'One minute she was there…' She sighed, thinking of the other young villagers who had vanished. 'Whatever happened to her, it wasn't the monster,' she added, as gently as she could, though she knew it must be of little comfort to Saul.

'And the Doctor?' asked Petr. 'Where is he?'

Martha turned to Saul. 'You saw the silver corridor?'

Saul nodded.

'That's where we came from. The Doctor went back. He can help us from there.'

'He's abandoned us,' said Petr, a self-pitying tone creeping into his voice.

'No,' said Martha firmly. 'The Doctor knows what he's doing. We have to trust him.'

'Why didn't you go with him?'

'I was worried for Saul,' said Martha. 'It looked like that dragon thing was going to finish him off. I couldn't just leave him…'

Saul bowed before Martha, his gratitude wordless once again.

'Neither could I,' said Petr simply. 'I had a sense something was… wrong. I came up to the forest and could hear things moving about. Creatures I did not recognise.'

Saul raised a quizzical eyebrow, but it was left to Martha to articulate his surprise. 'That doesn't sound much like you,' she said. 'Don't get me wrong, I'm grateful, but…'

'You think I am not by nature a man of action and instinct?' Petr glanced at his younger brother. 'You are right, but I had a good teacher.' A slow, sad smile passed over his features. 'You know, sometimes I can hear Saul's voice in my head, telling me about the plants, the animals, the web of life… Encouraging me to trust my instincts.'

Saul was preoccupied with the swords at his belt, studiously rearranging them so that he did not have to look his brother in the eye. 'If Jude has disappeared, like the others…' Saul sighed, a bleak note of defeat in his voice. He sounded crushed and resigned, as if the dragon had already stamped down on his body and ended his life.

'Look, if anyone can get to the bottom of the disappearances, it's the Doctor,' said Martha, desperate to offer Saul some hope. 'Whatever it is that generates and sustains this world – he'll find it, and make sure the children are brought back.'

Petr turned to look at Martha, his face grim. 'Tonight,

more and more people are seeing their children in the fog. The village is thick with innuendo and fear. If the legends are true, their return will only bring destruction to us all.'

Saul's face suddenly brightened; it was as if he'd been turning Martha's words over in his mind and now, finally, they had hit home. 'You said the Doctor is now in the place that sustains us all? Is that not the seat of the Creator, the place of the Eternal Dead?' His face broke into a grin, and it was a wonderful thing to see. 'Perhaps… perhaps Jude is with the Doctor.'

Petr laid a sympathetic hand on Saul's arm. 'Wherever Jude is… we must accept that we can't do anything for her now. I'm sorry.'

Martha was intrigued by Saul's sudden mention of some sort of religious belief; she was sure she had seen no churches in the village, and yet both men clearly shared a vocabulary that – however rarely used – required no further explanation.

She was about to question them on this when the dark silence of the forest was cut asunder by another piercing roar. At least one vast creature was moving towards them; Martha could hear the distant sound of trees toppling and being forced aside.

'What *are* those creatures?' asked Petr. He started to walk through the trees, towards the paths and tracks that led back to the village. To Martha's great relief, Saul was soon walking at his side.

'They mark the edge of our world,' said Saul simply. 'And our world is getting smaller all the time…'

'Where did you spring from?' exclaimed the Doctor, delighted. He'd given Jude a huge hug, and was now looking her up and down, amazed by her very presence on the research station.

'I don't know,' said Jude honestly. 'I was in the forest, then I was here! I woke up in a dark room. I think I fell.'

'You're so lucky!' exclaimed the Doctor. 'The barriers between our two worlds were breaking down. You could so easily have ended up in space, or just been snuffed out like a candle – but here you are! Large as life and twice as wonderful!' He looked around slowly, as if the full implication of his own words was only just dawning on him. 'Here you are… in the real world,' he whispered quietly. 'How is that even possible?'

'I didn't mean to go into the forest,' continued Jude, glancing around guiltily. 'I've only ever gone there with Dad before – he's always telling me it's not safe. But I wanted to see what you all were talking about. I wanted to say goodbye to you properly.'

'And instead you stumbled into that monster!'

'I've never seen anything like it!' said Jude, wide-eyed.

'Like so much of your world,' said the Doctor, 'it's as if countless legends and fables have been simmered down, condensed, puréed together in a blender…'

'Is my father going to be all right?'

'Martha went after him,' said the Doctor. 'I'm sure they'll be fine.'

'Where are we?' asked Jude. 'All I've seen so far are little rooms and long corridors. I've been wandering about for *ages*, but I can't work out what sort of building we're in.'

'We're in… a ship, I suppose you could say. The *Castor*, it's called – part prison, part science lab. We're drifting in deep space, millions of miles from the nearest planet. Your world, your home… well, it's sort of generated by this ship, and contained within it.' He sighed. 'That was gobbledegook, wasn't it?'

Jude nodded. 'You wouldn't make a very good teacher,' she said, giggling.

'Ah, well,' said the Doctor, feigning hurt. 'I'm more of a… hands-on kind of teacher, you know. I'd much rather show you something and let you make up your own mind.' He paused, thinking, then dashed off down the corridor, Jude close behind. He found a window, sealed shut, and operated a control at its base. The shutter slid open, revealing the haunting beauty of the profound darkness of space beyond.

Jude's eyes widened. She stared in silent and wondrous awe, allowing the Doctor to walk quietly back to the computer screen. He busied himself at the keyboard for a while, trying to reassure baffled software and overwrite recalcitrant protocols. Then he became aware of Jude's presence at his side.

After just a moment or two of confusion, Jude seemed to have understood where she was and what the Doctor was trying to show her. The girl was unflappable. 'And what's that?' she said calmly, pointing at the computer console.

'It shows me every living thing on this ship,' said the Doctor. He pointed to the intermittent, contradictory reading. 'This signal's puzzling. The systems can't get a lock on it, as if it doesn't really exist in this universe.'

'When I was wandering around,' said Jude, 'I kept seeing something out of the corner of my eye. I'd hear movement, but there was no one there.'

The Doctor looked up and down the long, bare corridor. Was it his imagination, or was it starting to become dark? Shadows seemed to be pooling at either end, and the doors recessed into the walls were much less clear now.

He turned back to the screen. He followed the signal along a corridor, tracing its path with his finger.

'Whatever it is,' said the Doctor, a note of anxiety creeping into his voice, 'I think it's coming this way.'

Martha, Petr and Saul returned to the village as quickly and as calmly as they could. Saul, not surprisingly, kept glancing over his shoulder, as if he thought he might catch some glimpse of his departed daughter. Martha didn't blame him; she wished there was more they could have done, but she had to admit she was glad to be leaving the dark trees and the sounds of gathering beasts far behind.

All three skidded to a halt when they finally emerged from the trees, amazed and disturbed by what they saw. Martha had encountered nothing like it before; down below them the village was entirely shrouded in fog. It had rolled in towards the clustered buildings from the lake and surrounding fields, and coagulated and coalesced in every space. Great blocks of mist pressed tightly against every window, every door; from a distance it appeared to be a solid, seemingly impenetrable bank of cloud, about three storeys high and almost exactly the same size and shape as the village. Above the village, and around it, the air seemed relatively clear and open.

Martha suppressed a shiver; Saul and Petr exchanged a glance, then began to jog down the path and towards the blanketed buildings.

They made their way to Saul's house. The fog was so thick Martha could only just make out her own hands in front of her face when she raised them. Thankfully Saul's instincts were unaffected, and Martha grabbed a fistful of his clothing from time to time for fear of losing him completely in the mist. But Saul's house was both empty and in darkness – and, now they looked more attentively through the fog, they could not see a single light burning against the grey fog.

'They've all gone!' exclaimed Petr, but Saul wasn't so quick to come to a judgement. He knocked loudly on his neighbours' homes – no response – and then set off down the mist-shrouded streets. Sighing, Martha and Petr ran after him.

They passed numerous silent houses, each a solid block of darkness that loomed suddenly out of the grey mist like a geometric creature of nightmare; the fog was so thick it soaked up every footfall, every sound of exertion, and even Saul's bold cries.

Suddenly, Petr stumbled over something – Martha wasn't surprised, even their feet and the ground on which they ran were barely visible. She bent down to help the village leader to his feet. Ignorant of their plight, Saul continued on and had soon disappeared into the grey, writhing void.

Something brushed against Martha's back. She turned instinctively.

A child stood some metres away, the fog surrounding him like a protective cocoon. Martha was about to cry out to the others when she suddenly noticed that the child's eyes were blank and lifeless, the colour of tears and slate and rain. The child's skin was pallid, but the entire figure was so pale you could hardly tell where skin ended and clothing began. If it were possible to sculpt a human form from fog, this would be the result.

The child extended an arm and reached out for Martha, its mouth opening soundlessly.

'Thom!' exclaimed Petr. He stumbled forward, almost falling to his knees again, but, like Martha, his initial reaction of delight soon turned to ice-cold fear when he stared into the boy's empty eyes.

'Come on!' said Martha, pulling Petr to her side and then propelling both of them deeper into the fog. Pure, primal terror took over. Martha wouldn't look back on her flight from the child with any degree of pride, but there was something so fundamentally lifeless about the figure that dread was the only natural response.

For the first time, Martha could hear her footsteps – or was it her heart beating? – as they put as much distance as they could between themselves and the phantasm. Petr was holding on to Martha tightly, as if he were a drowning man in a foaming sea of grey and Martha was the only thing that would keep him from going under.

Martha glanced back over her shoulder. The figure was fading away – first a smudged child's drawing, then an optical illusion caused by the writhing, overlapping banks of fog.

'This way!'

Saul's voice was strong enough to cut through even their terror; Martha and Petr half-ran, half-stumbled in the direction of the sound, an aural beacon in the silent nothingness of the fog. Moments later they saw the first glimmer of light, then the huge, resolute form of Saul. It seemed at first that Saul was holding back the fog by the sheer power of his presence; then Martha saw where they were.

The village hall was surrounded by light – every

lantern, every blazing torch from the village had been brought here and placed around the building. Every door, every window, every spare patch of ground front and back had a light hanging there; it was just enough to keep the fog at bay.

Behind Saul, in the huge arched doorway, stood the stooped figure of the Dazai, a lopsided grin on her lined face; behind her clustered a gaggle of villagers, looking out at the fog in terror.

'I thought,' said the old woman, taking a step towards Petr, 'that, in your absence, *someone* ought to take charge…'

The Doctor turned to Jude. 'Now, I don't want to worry you or anything,' he said, 'but there's no point hiding. I've been watching for this thing for some time and… Well, it seems quite capable of walking through doors and walls if the mood takes it.'

'And that's *not* worrying?' said Jude.

'The Doctor ruffled her hair like an overenthusiastic uncle, 'Don't worry. I'll think of something.'

'*We'll* think of something,' said Jude, emphatically. 'Anyway, how do you know this thing is evil?'

The Doctor sighed. 'When you've wandered the universe as long as I have,' he said, 'you can count the creatures that skulk about in the dark that are actually pleased to see you on the fingers of one hand. A Ralafean's hand, come to that.'

Jude looked at him blankly.

'The people of Ralafea,' explained the Doctor patiently. 'Notorious throughout the cosmos for having four thumbs and one finger per hand. Invented the mobile phone before the printing press. Anyway...' He took one last look at the screen – the creature or person or whatever was only a few metres away now, but apparently one floor beneath them. 'Thankfully, I want to go in the opposite direction. The main science hub.' He walked away, and Jude was forced to jog to keep at his side. 'I can't avoid the creature, so I might as well just go about my business...'

'What do you expect to find in this "hub"?' asked Jude.

'Lots and lots of answers,' said the Doctor. 'Big, juicy ones you can really get your teeth into.' He nodded back at the computer station. 'Just a dumb terminal, you see. Would only tell me so much.'

The Doctor's eyes narrowed – there seemed to be a dark shadow, overlaid on the computer terminal. The Doctor blinked, and the shadow vanished – just a plain, boring computer keyboard and screen set into the wall.

'Phew,' said the Doctor, increasing his walking pace just a little. 'Thought we were in trouble for a moment then.'

And, without really seeing it, he walked straight into the creature in front of him and was swallowed by darkness.

ELEVEN

Children are supposed to bring people together, not drive them further apart. At least, that was what Ben Abbas had always been taught. Now, locked in a marriage he did not understand, and saddled with a baby who seemed to demand constant attention and gave nothing back in return, Abbas wasn't sure of anything any more.

Abbas wondered – just for a moment – if he could gain any insight from looking at his father's life, but he quickly discounted the notion. His own father had been a bully and a cheat; it was a happy family only on the surface, with each of them playing set roles with the skill of trained actors. Any dissent, any *honesty* even, had been beaten out of them with simple precision.

Abbas was going to have to sort this out for himself. He was on his own. He smiled. Just like the old days…

He called out for Gabby Jayne – habit, as much as

anything else. He knew she was on a shoot until evening, and their son was safely tucked up at the nursery until four. So, time to get the evening meal on – and time to think.

Abbas wandered into the kitchen with a bag of vegetables, arranging them across the work surface once the automatic lights had flickered on. He turned to operate the control pad in the arched doorway, switching on the under-floor heating and making sure the screen in the wall was on the news channel.

He paused for a moment, letting the white noise of babbling voices wash over him, trying to force himself to relax, to get a grip on his emotions. OK, so she'd been spotted on the arm of that good-looking young actor with the famously unruly hair. It didn't amount to anything, did it? Perhaps Gabby Jayne was just doing what she was told, putting her face about a bit for the paparazzi – by all accounts, the boy was a rising star, and the soap in which he appeared had been the number one show for months. Not that Abbas had ever seen it, of course – he had better things to do with his time than watch fictional people betray and humiliate each other. He got enough of that in real life.

Still, perhaps it was time for a peace offering – one of his special lasagnes normally did the trick. 'Diplomats from the Pacific Rim Cooperative have told reporters that they hope that the leaders of the sub-Saharan autonomies will listen to their plans for a cessation of violence. World Minister Cho stated that the nations "need a period of peace, for the good of all our peoples".'

Abbas snorted, thinking still of Gabby Jayne. 'Yeah,' he said. 'That's what we need. Peace.'

As he began slicing an onion – the control panel chirruped, offering to prepare the vegetables for him, but Abbas preferred to do it the old way – the reporter handed back to the studio.

'Thanks, Benoit,' said the male anchor, turning to the camera with a well-practised smile. 'And now, other news... Scientists working at the New Rome Institute have announced that they are continuing with their controversial Chimera Project, despite opposition from human rights activists and prison reform groups. The project, which aims to rehabilitate dangerous offenders through extreme psychological processes, has been criticised for legitimising torture, and for its unusual methodology.'

Abbas reached for another onion. Though his eyes were streaming, he could just make out some sort of space station on the screen set into the wall; it spun on its axis against a milky background of bright stars and interstellar gas.

Despite everything, despite all these attempts to get Gabby Jayne out of his mind, Abbas' mind was bursting with images of her: when they first met, their honeymoon of unseasonal rain and midnight encounters in deserted restaurants, her first big break and all the joy that had brought them… His fingers almost slipped off the knife he was using.

Blasted onions!

The newsreader continued reading the autocue as smoothly as if the words were only now occurring to him. 'Concern has also been expressed as the research station *Castor*, and the Chimera Project it houses, is effectively beyond Earth jurisdiction. The station currently hangs in the demilitarised zone, though recently it had to call on Earth security forces to quell an uprising. All attempts at independent investigation have been rebuffed, and rumours of unacceptably high numbers of patient casualties persist.'

The newsreader paused, the smile becoming wider. 'Entertainment news, now, from Richard Sistrah. And, Richard, what's this I hear about young David Lotus considering turning his back on acting for another tilt at the music charts…?'

Abbas' knife slipped again, this time skidding across the worktop and sliding into his left hand.

'Ow!' exclaimed Abbas, automatically sucking his injured finger. The news footage muted, the systems seeming to have recognised his discomfort. The newsreader and the entertainment expert – a tall, gauche man perched uncomfortably on the edge of a desk – continued to converse with pre-planned joviality, their voiceless lips flapping vacantly.

The image switched again – a stock footage photo of the young actor, with Gabby Jayne on his arm.

Abbas peered more closely. Gabby Jayne was wearing her new dress – she'd only bought it the other day. That meant she was still seeing the little twerp!

Abbas stared at the blood that coursed down his finger, gripping the handle of the knife more tightly. Bolognese? A peace offering?

No. He had a better idea.

It was crowded inside the hall, the warm air scented with bodies and candlelight and fear. In the centre of the great chamber lay the village's children, huddled together under a patchwork of blankets and cloaks. They fidgeted constantly, tired but rarely willing or able to submit to sleep. Around the edge of the room, in a great protective circle, stood anxious parents. They gathered in small groups, whispering quietly and glancing out through the windows, where fingers of fog caressed and gripped the cold glass in an unending embrace. Others – those bereaved, those overcome by the terror of it all – sat huddled under shrouds, moaning and inconsolable as cold tears fell sluggishly from their eyes. Almost everyone was carrying some sort of lantern, gripped tightly in desperate fingers and held close as if afraid the mist would penetrate even here.

Martha, Saul and Petr followed the Dazai as she walked unsteadily through the hall. 'As the fog came in,' she explained, 'more children disappeared. At least four, in a single night! What's worse, more and more people are seeing their dear departed in the fog.' She paused for a moment, running her hands over the top of her cane, lost in thought. 'Whatever we think of the legends, it is clear that this fog is not natural. It seems to take away the living, and then return them to us as pale shadows. We had to do something!'

'And the light seems to keep the fog at bay,' said Martha.

The Dazai nodded. 'I decided we should all gather here. Since then, no one has disappeared, but the fog... It grows thicker all the time.'

Petr was about to ask a question of the Dazai when suddenly a woman ran across the room towards Saul. She almost threw herself at him, her panicked, exhausted voice waking those few children that slept. 'Where have you been? Where's Jude?' she screamed, on the verge of hysteria.

Saul pulled the woman tight to him, shushing her and stroking her hair. 'Sara, Sara, Sara,' he whispered.

'Where is she?'

Saul shook his head great head slowly. 'I'm sorry. She followed me into the forest. She must have sneaked out of the house...'

'What happened?'

'We were attacked... And Jude disappeared.'

'The fog took her?'

Saul shook his head again, more firmly now. 'No. No one saw what happened.'

The woman began to wail again, beating her fists feebly against Saul's great chest – as if she blamed him for everything that had happened. 'Jude!' she cried. 'Jude!'

'We'll find her, Sara,' said Saul, his voice now a croaked whisper. He turned to Petr, his eyes pleading. 'Won't we?'

Petr averted his gaze. He turned away after a moment, muttering, 'I need to organise a headcount.'

Kristine anxiously approached her weeping sister-in-law and placed an uncertain arm around the convulsing woman. Martha tried as best she could to comfort Sara. 'The Doctor has disappeared as well,' she said. 'But I know where he's gone. He's going to sort all this out. I promise.'

The woman looked at Martha through tear-smudged eyes. 'You cannot promise for another,' she said simply. 'You cannot promise when no one knows what is happening.'

Saul placed an arm around Sara, drawing her tightly to his chest, and Martha was left standing on her own in the centre of the hall, feeling powerless and sad.

The judge leaned forward, his thin lips pursed. 'Ben Abbas, is there anything you would like to say, either in your defence or in mitigation?'

'Plenty,' said Abbas. The guards on either side of him released their grip and let him stand.

Abbas took a moment to survey the courtroom, from the cameras and journalists up in the gallery, to the legal teams and jurors arranged in rows in front of him. So many faces, so many people eager to hear what he had to say – he would be famous, for a day or two at least.

He swallowed hard. Suddenly, the idea of his face, his words, being transmitted across the world on all the news channels seemed a little daunting. Still, he didn't have many fears left now. Better just tackle this as he tackled everything – head-on.

'She deserved it,' he said simply.

There was a sharp intake of breath from the jurors, the whine of cameras and recorders up in the gallery.

'Yeah,' he said. 'You heard me. She deserved it. You lot reckon she was all sweetness and light, but you never had to live with her!' He was warming to his theme already, using his hands to underline his points. 'One minute she's doing some interview, promoting her latest film and talking about her charity work and how she's the underclass's sweetheart, an inspiration to millions.' Abbas paused, taking a swig of water from the bottle at his side. 'Next, she's home with me, boasting about her latest boyfriend and wondering what shade of purple her next quad-fuel car's gonna be.'

'I'm not sure this is helping!' hissed the brief at his side, but it was too late now.

'She was always rubbing my nose in it – her wealth, how desirable she was… She said I was pathetic. Well, I showed her, didn't I?'

The judge's patience had long since snapped. 'That's enough,' he called out.

Immediately the guards were at Abbas' side, clamping his arms in their vice-like grip.

The judge, like a black vulture on a roost, peered down at the defendant. 'Benjamin Michael Abbas, you are an evil man. In your younger days, many people thought of you as a likeable rogue, a man who fraternised with gangsters but was beyond their despicable methodology. In fact, while imprisoned awaiting trial for the murder of your wife, the actress Gabby Jayne Hughes, you did finally admit to your role in a number of murders across many territories of the world. You cannot put these crimes down to the indiscretions of youth – these are murders, not acts of petty vandalism! And, though you did not kill these people yourself, by your actions you ensured that it was as if the finger on the trigger was yours.'

The judge sighed theatrically. 'You said you hoped to "turn over a new leaf" on your marriage to Miss Hughes. Instead, you became jealous of her, and of her work, and you even came to doubt that you were the father of your child. The "mitigating circumstances" quoted in your defence are excuses, mere flim-flam, designed to delay the execution of justice. Now, however, a court has found you guilty of cold-blooded and heartless murder.'

The judge paused, adjusting his wig for the benefit of the cameras. 'In this territory, we do not sentence to death. However, you will be imprisoned until death occurs. There will be no repeal, no reprieve, no hope of release.' His words fell heavily on the courtroom; even the excited, titillated whispers from the gallery faded away, replaced only with sonorous silence.

'However,' the judge continued, his eyes continuing to bore into Abbas' skull, 'in view of the severity of your crime, and your absolute lack of remorse, I will be recommending that you be forwarded to the deep-space correctional programme. Either the *Castor* or the *Pollux* will be a suitable final destination for you.'

'Just send me to prison!' exclaimed Abbas suddenly, his voice cracking. 'Don't send me there!'

The judge paused, glancing down at some notes. 'You showed no remorse towards your victim, and deliberately misled the subsequent police investigation. You are a man entirely lacking in compassion, pity and forgiveness. You have forced civilised society to treat you in the same way. I can show you no pity, no compassion – nor would I want to. Benjamin Michael Abbas, you are evil, and a menace to all right-thinking people. I'm pleased to say that no one in this room will ever have to see your face again.'

He paused, then nodded to the guards.

'Take him down.'

* * *

Martha nodded in the direction of Saul's wife. Sara was motionless now, as if in a trance, her eyes looking into the middle distance and seeing nothing.

'How is she?'

Kristine shrugged. 'You always think your own child is going to be safe – even if everyone around you is in danger, you think, you hope, you pray... that you're uniquely blessed – or that your children are, at least.' Kristine glanced down. 'When we lost Thom...'

'I'm sorry,' said Martha, knowing the words were inadequate but not knowing what else to say.

Kristine stared at the candle that guttered and spat on the table at her side. She and Martha had found a quiet corner close to Saul and Petr, who stood whispering. Occasionally their voices rose in disagreement, but mostly their heads were together, conspiratorial and anxious.

'Thom's first word,' said Kristine, indicating the candle, and the starscape of lanterns that flickered the length and breadth of the room. '*Light!* He just came out with it one day. I was sitting down to bathe him, and was just pouring some water when he pointed at a candle. "Light!" he said, as clear as day, and then he gave me the biggest smile you can imagine. He could be difficult – all children have their moments! – but for the rest of that day he seemed content, as if he'd done all he set out to.'

Martha thought of family gatherings, of weddings and parties terrorised by out-of-control children – but knew that any parent, for all their scolding and exasperation, would be hurt beyond words if the boy or girl were suddenly snatched from them. 'You must miss him awfully,' she said, again cursing her bedside platitudes but not sure she had the vocabulary for anything else.

Kristine nodded silently. Martha rested a hand on Kristine's arm.

'I'm intrigued,' said Martha. 'You said you prayed for Thom's safety. Saul said something about a place where you believe the dead go… But I haven't seen any churches here.'

Kristine smiled. 'We believe in a church not made with hands,' she said simply. 'What sustains us is everywhere, and in everything – or it's nowhere at all.'

Martha nodded, thinking of the Doctor on the *Castor*, wondering if he had yet discovered who – or what – had created, and was now sustaining, this bubble of life. For all the Doctor's talk of the unreality of this place, she couldn't help but think of everyone that surrounded her as being real. When you're presented with suffering, she thought to herself, you react to it on a human level – with sympathy. You'd be something less than human if you didn't. And did it really matter that these people had been birthed by some sort of technology locked away in a human space station that they had never seen? They had grown, evolved, matured – seemingly become sentient and able to love and hate in equal measure – and she could not abandon them now.

Martha got to her feet, desperate to do something, desperate to make things better for the people around her. She moved past the stiff and upright form of Sara, who shuddered silently, her arms still wrapped around her own body in a meaningless embrace.

'Welcome to hell,' said the guard, without a trace of irony in his voice.

Abbas watched the plasteel door seal itself shut. Moments later, the red warning light over the airlock flicked on; he felt the floor shake slightly as the transport ship disengaged from the larger craft. Through the window he could just make out the flash of a silver wing as the transporter banked. Without warning – and in absolute silence – the big engines flared for an instant, causing Abbas to blink involuntarily.

When his eyes opened again the ship was nowhere to be seen, lost in the fathomless darkness of space. It was as if the captain couldn't stand to be in this sector any longer than he absolutely had to.

Abbas didn't blame him. He'd heard the rumours about this place, and none of them were pleasant.

'This way,' said the guard, his eyes full of longing as he averted his gaze from the spot where the transport vessel had been.

Abbas tried to swallow down the irrational, claustrophobic feeling that had gripped him from the first moment he'd glimpsed the research station.

He followed the guard, shuffling through the angular corridor, passed a number of bright-white rooms, then stepped out onto the latticed walkway that encircled the small communal area. Looking down he could see a handful of overall-clad men training with weights or sparring in a hastily assembled ring of plastic crates and thick rope. It was clear from the light-emitting signs that peppered the walls that the door at the far side of the walkway led to the security team's sleeping and social quarters. To his left, endless, anonymous cells. To his right, the technical area – the heart of the ship, and Abbas' eventual destination.

Before he stepped off the curved walkway and into the antiseptic corridor, Abbas risked a glance upwards. Through the thick, transparent bubble that formed the roof of the common room, he could see a planet, impossibly close, impossibly large. Its pale blue mass seemed to threaten to hurtle downwards at any moment, its landmasses and frozen oceans ravenous for the microscopic morsel that was the research centre.

Abbas glanced away as his head and stomach swam with the unnaturalness of it all. Heaven above, hell below, he thought. There was something primal about the arrangement.

The guard caught his hasty look at the planet. 'I know,' he said quietly. 'Does my head in, too.'

As they walked along the featureless corridor, Abbas felt the faintest of vibrations through the floor, as if they were approaching some sleeping creature. Every ten metres or so they passed a door, numbered and with a status panel at head height. On some the digits were green; others, blue; still others, a twinkling scarlet. As they passed each red door, and despite the soundproofing, Abbas could hear muffled screams and cries of anguish.

They came to a halt about halfway down the long corridor. The shouts from the next room were just reaching a crescendo, the red lettering spelling out words and numbers that Abbas couldn't follow. Then, suddenly, there was silence. The read-out cycled though amber, then blue, then finally became green.

The door began to hiss open, but Abbas was bundled into his own room before he could see who or what emerged.

'Sit down,' said a bald, white-coated man, indicating a padded seat of synthetic leather in the centre of the room. His manner was imperious and abrupt, as if he did not expect to be challenged. The guards on either side of him, armed with snub-nosed guns, showed that the scientist had every reason to be confident.

Within moments, Abbas found himself strapped to the seat, utterly unable to move. The white-coated man turned his back for a moment, his hands moving over a pedestal of equipment. Then he turned towards Abbas, a wicked smile on his face.

'This is the point,' he said, 'when convention dictates

that I should say that it won't hurt a bit.' He leant closer, and Abbas could feel his breath on his cheek. 'But I don't like lying…'

And, within moments, Ben Abbas *was* in hell.

Martha approached Petr and his younger brother. 'What are we going to do?' she asked, impatiently. She hadn't risked life and limb to save Saul from the monster in the forest just to sit in a hut all night.

Petr looked back at her, uncertain. 'The Dazai says that since she moved everyone in here no child has gone missing.'

Martha remembered the Doctor talking about the blank pages in the Dazai's books. If there was only so much memory to go round, it might account for the creatures at the forest's edge. They were there to prevent Saul or anyone else from travelling too far. It might also make sense of the strictures that the village had always placed on Saul – a traveller, a questing spirit, prevented from exploring too deeply into the forest, or from travelling to the centre of the lake at all. It might even explain the fog, and the disappearing children, and how everything seemed to have stabilised since the villagers had gathered in the great hall. In going into the forest, Martha, Saul and Petr had also been pushing at the boundaries of this world; now they had returned, and everything had stabilised.

Still, Martha wasn't prepared to just wait for the

Doctor to sort things out from his end. She had to do something – she had to find out what had happened to all the children. She couldn't stand looking at the empty, drained faces of Kristine and Sara, and having only meaningless words to offer them in return.

She wasn't sure how much she could share with the others – about the fog, and the borders of their enclosed world, and the disappearances. And, even if she could convince them of these things, whether it would help or hinder their progress towards a solution to their problem.

'There must be a way to get the children back,' suggested Martha carefully.

Petr seemed unconvinced. 'We should attend to the torches, get as much sleep as we can – wait for daybreak.'

Martha imagined that the more people that slept, the more likely the world was to shut down entirely. 'I don't think that's such a good idea,' she said firmly – adding, in her own mind, *for me at least*.

The Dazai came over, her stick clicking on the flagstones. 'The girl may be right,' she said firmly. 'After the Doctor departed I consulted the legends – the source material, you might say, not what we remember of them.' She raised a quivering hand to forestall any objections. 'I know some of us do not accept that folk tales and ancient curses have any bearing on our lives,' she said, 'but consider what has happened so far. Our children have disappeared in the fog, and now they are returning – returning to enquire how well we treated them. Returning, as if to judge us: *Are we fit parents? Are we fit to live?* It all conforms to the tales we have told for generations. And, even if we choose not to accept the prophecies, the stories say that the fate of our village hangs in the balance.'

Martha stared out of the window, watching shapes moving through the fog. Martha blinked – just for a moment, she could have sworn she'd seen a boy, juggling shadows, but when she looked again it was just a curl of fog, animated only by a breath of wind.

'The stories may be a… reverse echo… of all that we have seen,' said the Dazai. 'And what may yet come to pass.'

'What are we going to do?' asked Martha again. She hadn't properly met the Dazai before, but she was impressed by the old woman's forthright, businesslike manner. Martha remembered the last time she'd seen her father's granny – a shrivelled old bean of a woman, mahogany-coloured and hat-wearing, but refusing to be dictated to by medical infirmity or wheelchair. The Dazai, the spiritual and philosophical heart of the village, reminded Martha of that old woman who, even when surrounded by death, was never less than full of life.

'There is something we can do,' said the Dazai firmly.

'Go back to the forest?' suggested Martha hopefully. 'The Doctor disappeared there, and I was thinking…'

The old woman shook her head. 'There is a better way. The island, in the heart of the lake…'

'But that's where the children are coming from!' exclaimed Petr – who seemed quite prepared to believe the legends now.

'On the island, there is a cave, and within the cave, is the monster – not those small beasts that patrol the forests, but the god-monster that drives the children towards us. The stories say that all shall *not* be lost if a brave hero ventures there to slay the evil.'

Saul grinned, and Martha noticed him grasp the hilt of his sword ever more tightly. The Dazai looked from Saul to Petr. 'Of course, in the original text, the number of heroes is not specified.'

And then she turned to Martha.

'And neither is the gender.'

Abbas sat alone in the dark, his knees pulled up to his chest, and remembered. He thought of the brief moments of happiness that had punctured his life, the jealousy that had almost sent him mad – his attempt to cook a meal for Gabby Jayne. How pathetic! Then the televised trial, complete with preening judges and jurors. After the trial had come the long trip to the research station *Castor*, way out in neutral space and beyond the reach of any meaningful legislation.

He remembered his first day on the station – the guard who'd welcomed him to hell, the smell of fear and disinfectant that seemed to hang heavy in the air – and the unremitting torture that began moments after his arrival. It was torture, of course – there was no other way of looking at it, however hard the jailers and the scientists tried to apply the masquerade of science and research. It hurt physically, of course – each session was like a trip to the electric chair, the 'Mercy Seat' of old Earth penitentiaries, but without the finality – and release – of death at its conclusion. But, worse than that, was the emotional trauma, of literally reliving every bad experience, every moment of deceit, every murderous impulse – and, in his case, every murderous action.

And the dreams that followed… For weeks Abbas had dreamt of stabbing Gabby Jayne, again and again, over and over, and yet each night she was alive again, and Abbas was no longer sure what was nightmare and what was reality.

Eventually, though, progress had been made. Abbas began to forget his past, forget who he was – and it was not time that healed and erased his memories, but the machinery, the experiments. His memories – even his very personality and mind – were coming adrift, until everything in his head moved and changed position, like numerous icebergs sailing away from the landmass that had once sustained them all.

Day-to-day relationships with the other prisoners

were either strained or non-existent: with each person in their own private anguish, hell wasn't so much other people as yourself magnified. Hell was being forced forever to live in the past, to confront it – and then watch it drift away into the void of ambiguity. Hell was loneliness.

And now, as death closed in, Abbas felt more lonely than ever. He was on his own – most of the others were dead now – and he was absolutely powerless.

He looked about him – his cell door was open, either wrenched apart by some great force, or casually disengaged when the systems overloaded and fire swept through the technical areas. He could still smell the burning now – the rank bitterness of smouldering metal and flesh – and hear the screams of terror in his mind, even though that stage of the calamity had long since passed into awful silence. Screams of terror, as one man turned on another in a frenzy of violence. Some were driven to destroy – others to strive to survive at all costs.

Despite the open door, Abbas was sanguine and passive. Through the arch he could see the great curved cylinder of cells that formed this wing of the prison area. Fires flared in some, while outside others were crumpled black shapes, angular limbs jutting upwards like the residue of a forest after a lightning strike. One or two people moved about, from corridor to room to cell, crying and pitiful – at least, they had been people, once.

Now, robbed of their minds, robbed of all that made them human, they were merely units of biological noise and motion, waiting only for death.

And the killer that hunted in the shadows – indeed, was shadow itself – would embrace them all soon enough.

There was another sudden, sharp cry from somewhere, throttled away to a whisper within moments. Abbas got to his feet uncertainly, walked – as if a baby taking his first steps – out of his cell and to the handrail, and looked up and down the dizzying structure.

It was silent now, and motionless. He could hardly remember his crimes, and he did not know if he was *worse* than the others who had died, or better – or if it was just a random twist of fate that meant he was going to be the last human to look out at research station *Castor*.

Castor – the drive to tame wild things, now itself consumed by uncontrollable violence.

'Come on!' he shouted, his voice echoing around the caged void. 'I'm here! It's my turn!'

Abbas didn't want to be alone. He wasn't even sure he wanted to be human anymore.

The angel of shadow and death ascended majestically towards Abbas, in the central space between the floors and walkways and cells. It came towards him, illuminated by the flickering of the emergency lights. The creature was almost invisible and yet horrifyingly real.

There was a moaning sigh – the last thing Abbas realised was that he himself was making the noise – and the thing devoured him. Ben Abbas would neither live nor die nor be lonely ever again.

TWELVE

Jude saw the Doctor fall out of the shadow and into the light, clutching his chest and choking as if plucked from a dark sea.

Jude ran forward, wondering if she ought to clap him on the back to make sure he was breathing properly. 'Doctor!' she cried. 'Are you all right?'

The Doctor stood for a moment, obviously unsteady on his feet and breathing heavily. He looked around, sightless – and then hugged Jude tightly to him. 'Did you miss me?' he laughed, his face now flushed and full of colour.

'What happened to you?' asked Jude. 'That shadow thing seemed to suck you up, and then...'

'Then?'

'You were hanging there, hanging in mid air – and flailing around like you were having a bad dream!'

The Doctor took a step back, puffing his cheeks.

'Blimey,' he said, more quietly. 'The things I experienced in there… One man in particular – his entire life flashing before my eyes… And I felt every emotion as he did. All the terrible things he had done…' The Doctor paused. 'He was the last man to die. It was as if the creature was trying to show me something – trying to give me an insight into what went on here…'

'I don't understand, Doctor,' said Jude. 'What was that creature?'

'It was… a thousand nightmares made flesh,' said the Doctor, but then he immediately shook his head, irritated with himself. 'No, no, no, that's not the best way of putting it. It's like… you ever watched your mum make, oh I don't know, chicken stock or something?'

Jude found herself nodding, desperate not to interrupt the Doctor's flow.

'You chuck in bones and flesh and herbs and, you know, bit of white wine maybe… and you carefully boil it – not too hot, mind, you want to do it to last as long as possible – and then you start to filter away all the bones and the fat and gunk…'

'And you're left with something yummy and concentrated, like chicken multiplied by chicken,' suggested Jude, breathless.

'Exactly,' said the Doctor. 'Chicken squared – the very *essence* of chicken.' His face darkened. 'Only this thing, this creature… It's not good at all. It's as if all humanity is thrown into a pot and, after decades, all that's left… is evil. Pure, unthinking, unadulterated evil.'

'But why?'

'This is a prison ship,' said the Doctor simply. 'There were evil men here…'

Jude still wasn't sure she understood. 'But what happened when the creature swallowed you?'

'I experienced every bad feeling, every bad action ever committed by the people who were here. Memories, desires, impressions… It made the prisoners go mad. What was worse, I could feel it tugging at my own mind… My own past.' A distant look came into the Doctor's eyes. 'The things I've seen,' he added in a whisper. 'The things I've endured, the things I felt I had to do… I wouldn't want to share them with *anyone*.' He managed a weak smile. 'But this creature was just *desperate* for all of my memories. Didn't ask for permission, didn't check with me first – just went straight for the file marked *Private, No Admittance*.' He paused. 'Most people would have died.'

'So why didn't it kill you?' asked Jude simply.

'That's a very good question,' said the Doctor. 'I think there's even more going on here than meets the eye. Something else, some…' Jude watched him look around, at the metal corridor, and the junctions and rooms that extended off from it. It seemed a little brighter again, now that the shadow creature had gone, but Jude knew that it should be night. The lights that blazed in the ceiling could not be trusted to burn forever.

'We've got to find the heart of this station,' said the

Doctor. 'Somewhere, at its core, are all the answers we need.'

'The hub you spoke of,' said Jude.

The Doctor nodded, then stepped forward confidently. 'It's this way.'

'You sure? Looks to me like you're going the wrong way.'

'No, it's over here…'

Moments later, he doubled back on himself. 'We were going the wrong way,' he said simply. 'I reckon if we go down here we might avoid the creature.'

'Why?'

'I'm not sure I'll be so lucky if it attacks me again,' said the Doctor. 'Believe it or not, this place is like heaven to your world,' he added, casually, a few moments later. 'It's the God Particle that exploded it into life. It shapes it, guides it, influences it. And if there's a battle in heaven between – let's not be modest! – good and evil…' He smiled again, a grim smile, like a commander on the eve of war. 'You can guarantee there'll be a battle in your world as well.'

The lights chose that very moment to dim, the entire corridor suddenly taking on a dusky feel.

'Come on,' said the Doctor. 'We haven't got long.'

Martha stood outside the meeting hall, grateful to be away from its oppressive heat and the almost palpable sense of anxiety and dread. She glanced up at the sky.

'Strewth!' she exclaimed in surprise.

'What is it?' asked Saul.

Martha pointed upwards – it was like looking through a grey, misty tunnel that eventually faded away to show the dark night sky. And what a sky it was – absolutely clear of cloud, and absolutely free of stars and moon. There seemed to be no substance to it whatsoever. Beyond the village, it seemed, was absolutely… nothing.

'The destruction of the village comes closer,' said Petr.

'We'd better get cracking, then,' said Martha, trying to counter the leader's melodrama with an assured tone.

Holding their lanterns aloft, they began to edge forward. The fog seemed to split apart as they neared, driven back by their presence and by the light, and then flow back into place behind them. It surrounded them always, encircling a rough cylinder of light with Martha and the two brothers at the centre. Houses appeared in the mist as dark, angular shapes. Given what had happened to the night sky, Martha wasn't entirely convinced they'd resolve themselves into buildings if they stepped any closer.

Regardless, they stuck to the path between the buildings, which wound its way from the centre of the village and towards the lake. They passed over a tiny bridge, arched like something from an oriental garden, and Martha noticed that it was drained of colour, the wood appearing misshapen and unfinished.

If Saul and Petr noticed any changes to their village, they said nothing, and continued walking forwards, heads bowed as if in prayer – or fear.

'How much further?' asked Martha.

'It's not far,' said Saul.

'There are some boats moored up behind Carlo's home,' said Petr, as usual less reserved than his brother. 'He's one of the few brave enough to fish the waters of the lake.'

'Brave enough?'

'The legends,' said Saul. 'The fog, the children… The island. They're always linked.'

'If the lake so terrifies you, why do you stay?'

Petr glanced at Martha, clearly puzzled. 'You don't have to *believe* in legends and stories,' he said, 'to treat the lake with respect.'

'It seems calm enough,' said Martha, though in truth it was still hidden from her by the fog, and she was simply remembering how she had last seen it – and how it had seemed ever since her arrival. It was a great mirror of a lake, flat and serene but for the occasional gust of wind that skipped over its surface.

Petr and Saul exchanged a look, though they said nothing.

Martha was about to press them on the subject when a dark form appeared in the fog in front of them. The shape of a teenager or a small adult, it was smudged and blurred by the mist that cocooned it.

Yet, somehow, Petr recognised something about the indistinct figure – some indefinable quality that went beyond mere physical or visual recognition. 'Thom!' he cried, running forward – dodging Saul's outstretched arms and ignoring the big man's cry of 'No, Petr – no!'

Petr, dropping his lantern in his headlong rush, threw himself into the arms of the boy – only to find himself embracing nothing more than droplets of water and air. Petr fell to his knees, sobbing.

Martha ran to Petr's side, but Saul was motionless. His head scanned quickly from side to side. He was, Martha supposed, in hunting mode, his senses alert and his body tense.

Behind them – Saul was the first to notice, and he turned swiftly on the spot – the tall boy appeared again, more distinct now. The child's eyes, full of sorrow, burned like torches in the deepening gloom. 'Father,' he said, his voice as fragile as autumn leaves – but he was looking at Saul, not Petr.

Martha watched as Saul recoiled and took a sudden step backwards.

The effect on Petr was almost as immediate – he jumped to his feet, his slender hands wiping away his tears. 'I'm here, son,' he called, but it was in vain, for the ghostly figure ignored him, staring instead at Saul. 'Why were you never honest with Petr?' asked the child, taking another step forward. With each movement, the figure seemed to take on form and mass, as if the very fog was thickening and shaping life itself. He appeared to be a teenager, gangling and awkward, his face fixed in a bewildered frown.

'There are some things you don't want to say,' said Saul, staring only at his great hands, clasped as if in prayer. 'Some things… You want to leave unspoken.'

'Thom,' said Petr, naked desperation in his voice. 'It's me… Your father.'

Martha stood beside Petr, a sinking feeling in her stomach. 'You don't *know* that's Thom,' she said. 'It could just be… something sent to trick you.'

'You think I wouldn't recognise my own child?' Petr was furious now, though Martha realised he wasn't angry with her, but with the fact that the boy – apparently his son – was still ignoring him.

Still ignoring him, and addressing *Saul* as his father.

Saul looked up, staring into the soulless eyes of the young man before him. 'How did you find out?' he whispered. 'We never told you… We decided it would be too… damaging.'

'Damaging?' Petr sprang behind his brother, pulling him into a headlock, squeezing his neck with his long arms.

'No!' Martha threw herself at Petr, but the man brushed her aside easily. She fell forwards onto her face, tasting the grit of the path.

'I'm going to kill you,' said Petr with grim finality, tightening his grip on Saul's huge throat. Saul fell to his knees, his eyes bulging – and yet he did not struggle. He seemed entirely accepting of his fate.

Martha got to her feet, still swaying, and looked over at the ghostly boy – only to find that he had entirely disappeared. And, as the fog thickened and came closer all the time, the only sound she could hear was Saul, choking.

The Doctor was running at breakneck speed down a bewildering succession of corridors. Jude wasn't sure how much longer she could keep up with him. 'Humans!' he was exclaiming, still clearly irritated by what he had seen when the shadow creature had enveloped him. 'They are amazing. Absolutely amazing! But, my *god*, they can be thick!'

'What do you mean?' said Jude, struggling to breathe, talk and run all at the same time.

'Thinking they can do away with evil with the wave of a technological wand!' he exclaimed, suddenly coming to a halt before a great, rounded door and waving what seemed, to Jude's eyes at least, a technological magic wand in front of him. A panel set into the wall made a chirruping noise, and the door began to open. 'Evil isn't a *disease* you can eradicate just by messing with people's minds,' he continued, almost hopping from foot to foot like a child waiting to open an enormous wrapped gift. 'And you can't remove people's bad memories and somehow think that'll make everything *hunky dory*.'

He ducked through the doorway before it was fully open, and started running again. Jude noticed that there seemed to be fewer bodies in this part of the 'ship' – soon after the monster had attacked, they'd moved onto one of the 'habitation levels' and the signs of carnage had been all too apparent. The Doctor had tried to keep Jude from the worst of it, but even so both were much happier when they found their way into this section of the vessel, still gleaming and apparently new. 'Better seals on the doors,' the Doctor had explained absent-mindedly. 'A door a day… keeps decay at bay,' he'd added, nonsensically.

Nothing could disguise the fact that it was getting darker all the time – and, once or twice, Jude was sure there'd been something in her peripheral vision, lurking just out sight. The Doctor seemed attuned to the dwindling light, running faster and seeming to become yet more agitated with every passing moment. Jude kept trying to ask him questions, if only to slow him down a little. 'But surely,' she said, 'whether you had a nice childhood, how your parents treat you… Doesn't that change who you are?'

The Doctor beamed at Jude. He seemed pleased that she was able to follow what he was saying – and to engage with him. 'Evil actions are the result of *decisions*,' he was saying, forcefully. 'Not environmental factors, not genetics. They have their place, of course, but… You can't blame other people, other things, for what you do.

Two children, brought up in similar circumstances, don't end up as the same person! Your personality is the sum of everything that's happened to you, yes – but also of every decision you've made.'

He stopped suddenly, the corridors forming a crossroads. 'Talking of decisions… Which way?'

Jude shrugged.

'Haven't seen a map for a while,' explained the Doctor. 'I know it's not far, but…'

'That monster,' said Jude, still turning everything over in her mind. 'You said it's made up of all the evil thoughts of all the prisoners who were here…'

The Doctor nodded. 'Every thought, every instinct and desire…'

'So what was left behind?'

'Good question,' said the Doctor. 'After the treatment, were the prisoners truly human, were they capable of free will?' He looked around, and for a moment Jude imagined herself back on the walkways that connected the cells, with their bodies and piles of grey ash. 'Clearly not everything that's happened here is a result of this shadow creature. Some of what we've seen… Well, let's just say that the prisoners still had the capacity to choose to do wrong, to be selfish and violent when perhaps, had they joined together, sought refuge…'

'The Dazai says to choose is to be human.'

The Doctor smiled. 'Perhaps that's it… Perhaps that's what your entire world is.'

'What?' asked Jude.

'A place where human beings – even specially created ones – can struggle with issues of choice, of morality, of free will… An arena, a theatre stage, a science lab, all rolled into one. But why? Who benefits?'

'Doctor…'

'Hmm?'

'The choice before us… I know which way to go.'

'Really?'

Jude pointed – at the far end of the corridor they faced, where shadows thrived and merged, she could just make out the angelic creature that had attacked the Doctor.

'Any corridor but that one,' she said simply.

'He's gone!' shouted Martha. Desperate, she was trying to pull Petr's hands from his brother's throat. 'Your boy, Thom – he's disappeared!'

She tugged at Petr's arms, seemingly in vain. Though less well built than Saul, Petr was no desk-bound wimp. He was as strong as anyone in the village, given that all lived in harsh conditions and had to struggle to survive. Martha could barely get a grip on his arms, and she was worried that he might throw her aside again. Her lip was sore from where she'd hit the ground, and one hand and elbow were grazed.

'Gone?' said Petr suddenly. The manic look drained from his face like drawn poison. His arms dropped, limp, to his sides.

Saul collapsed, choking and gasping for air.

'You could have killed him!' said Martha, more angry now than anything. 'You stupid, stupid man! We've got to get to that island – *together*.'

Petr looked around, desperate to get one last glimpse of his son, but the wall of fog was opaque now. He looked down at his brother, though his eyes didn't seem to focus on him. 'We'll talk later,' he growled, and marched off into the fog.

Martha helped Saul to his feet. 'Is it true?' she asked, not sure if they should trust the apparition they had just seen. 'You and Kristine…'

Saul got up, looking guilty – and grateful to be alive. 'We've always been very close,' he explained, clearing his throat and dusting himself down. 'We saw each other for months before Petr even noticed her – always had his head in the clouds, you see. Even then.'

'And, even though she married Petr…'

'He's always been suspicious of me.'

'Sounds like he has every right to be,' said Martha. She didn't mean to be so harsh, but the last thing she needed – when the world was about to end – was a domestic feud. Saul said nothing in response.

They soon came across Petr, stooped by a handful of small boats that were moored behind a large house on stilts, right at the lake's edge. The fog was a little less thick here, and Petr was already waist-deep in the water, struggling to untie one of the boats.

Saul wordlessly waded into the lake, helping his brother with the rope, which was matted and the colour of algae. Soon both men were in the boat and trying to help Martha to join them without tipping the whole thing over.

Martha wasn't overly keen on ships of any size, still less this rickety vessel that seemed little more advanced than a coracle from a museum. It was far larger than she might have expected, though, with a definite prow and stern, and places set up for oars, and plenty of room in the centre for fish – or, in this case, a bedraggled woman convinced she'd left her sea legs behind. Martha flopped into the middle of the boat with all the grace and finesse of a harpooned seal.

As she struggled to sit, Saul and Petr began to row the boat across the lake. Without talking, without even looking at each other, they established a decent, sustainable rhythm. Soon the shoreline, and the cluster of shapes that represented the village, slipped back into the fog.

The boat lurched suddenly. Perhaps the lake wasn't as calm as it appeared.

'You said you had to be brave to fish in the lake,' said Martha. 'Why's that, then?' In truth, she was just desperate to break the silence that the brothers had lapsed into.

'Oh, you're safe enough if you stay near the shore,' said Saul, after a rare glance at Petr as if asking for permission to speak.

'Given that we're heading out towards the island,' said Martha, 'that doesn't entirely answer my question.'

'You'll find out soon enough,' said Saul. He turned his gaze back to the lake in front of him. The water was calm again, as flat as a sheet of glass, and the fog that drifted in streamers and strands around the boat seemed to soak up every noise, bar the occasional lap of water as the boat pushed on towards the island. The island began to solidify in the distance, a small, peaked black shadow wreathed with cloud.

'So,' said Martha. 'What's on the island?' She paused. 'Anyone?'

Saul and Petr said nothing, toiling away with the long wooden oars.

Martha sighed – it would have been nice to know what to expect, but she supposed it was going to be more monsters and beasts to mark the edge of this world. Perhaps it was just as well not to know.

She glanced back. The village was entirely out of sight now, the constantly moving fog expanding as far as she could see in every direction. She was grateful for Saul and Petr's competence – if it was down to her, they'd probably end up rowing around in circles.

This comforting thought faded from her mind the moment something hit the boat. It wasn't turbulence in the water, or the effect of a sudden squall of wind – a pale shape was moving through the dark waters.

Her blood ran cold. She looked over at the brothers, who'd scarcely missed a beat. 'What was that?' she asked.

'Just a friendly welcome,' said Saul. 'We'll only be in trouble if they all come at once.'

Saul's use of the plural bothered Martha almost as much as the idea of an attack on the boat. With great trepidation she peered over the side.

A handful of bullet-shaped creatures swam under the boat, their paths criss-crossing as they made powerful, darting surges forward. Martha thought at first that they were swelling and growing bigger. Then she realised that each one was rising up through the grey waters of the lake.

There was a sudden splintering sound only a few feet away from where Petr was patiently rowing. Through the shattered wood and turgid water Martha could see some sort of snout as a creature tried to widen the hole. It disappeared again and the boat began to fill with water.

There was another bump, then the entire craft started to shake wildly. Martha gripped the wooden rail that ran across the centre of the boat; it was like being thrown into a tumble dryer. The air was full of water as the boat flexed and twisted. Great waves threatened to flood it entirely.

Martha looked over the side again. More and more of the creatures were circling the boat, thrashing and writhing and clearly desperate to attack the vessel.

There was another sound of splintering wood.

'Right,' said Martha. 'I think we can safely say we're in trouble now.'

THIRTEEN

It was so dark on the *Castor* that the Doctor was using his wand – sonic screwdriver, he'd called it – to illuminate the corridors as they walked. They'd taken a circuitous route in an attempt to avoid the shadow creature, and the Doctor had filled in the silence by reminding Jude that the fate of her entire world might rest on how quickly they could find the heart of the ship.

Jude still wasn't sure she understood what the Doctor had said, but the gathering shadows were eloquent enough. A darkness was flowing over everything that Jude knew and took for granted. If the Doctor didn't succeed, Jude might never see the light again.

'You've got to hand it to Martha,' said the Doctor, seeming to move more slowly now for fear of stumbling over something in the dark. 'Whatever it is she's doing, it's just enough…'

'Just enough to what?'

'To give whoever it is that's sustaining your world something to think about. I'm sure your father's helping, too,' he added with a sympathetic smile.

'And if they stopped?'

The Doctor paused, his face hidden by shadow. 'Goodnight Vienna,' he said quietly. He pointed at the ceiling, where a row of lights still glowed faintly. 'Should be pitch black by now,' said the Doctor. 'By rights, your people should be asleep, and this place... This place should be as quiet as the grave.'

He paused, standing at another intersection, turning his head slowly as if listening for something.

'Whereas,' he said, excitement returning to his voice again, 'you just listen to that! The hum of machinery, the gentle vibration of electricity through circuit boards!'

Jude wasn't sure she could hear anything at all.

'This way!' said the Doctor urgently. 'Nearly there. Where there's noise there's...'

He stopped suddenly. A solid wall of shadow blocked the corridor in front of them; at its heart, like some great carrion bird flying against the wind, an ethereal figure hovered silently. A twisted angel, unfathomable and random and with no comprehension of what the Doctor was trying to do.

'We'll have to go back,' said Jude, grasping the Doctor's hand tightly.

'Can't,' said the Doctor simply. 'The control room, the heart of the ship... It's right over there.'

'But you said if we saw that thing again… it might kill us. It might drain us, or scare us witless, or…'

'You're young!' said the Doctor positively. 'How many bad things can you have done?'

'Enough,' said Jude.

'Even so,' said the Doctor, a stiffer determination in his voice now, 'we need to get to the door behind that creature.'

'You go,' said Jude, suddenly not feeling at all brave. 'I'll wait here.'

''Fraid I'm going to need your help,' said the Doctor in a whisper. 'I can't do it on my own.'

Jude paused, trying to make sense of everything. She supposed she was just a normal child, that she'd not done *much* wrong. She'd certainly never *deliberately* set out to bully or to hurt anyone. But if this creature was going to sift them both like wheat from chaff, was that enough? Her reading of books about morality indicated that there was more to a good life than an *absence* of evil. How many *positive* things had she actually done?

There was a beggar in the village, a scary old drunk with a habit of talking to himself and randomly shouting at the children as they played. Had she *ever* given him food or drink? Had she ever even tried to talk to him? And, even if she *had* – had she done it for the right reasons, or because people *expected* her to be good and kind? Did she hope for rewards when she did good deeds, or was she *truly* good?

Anyway, this monster of shadows… Who was to say its idea of good and evil was the same as hers? At school, she had a reputation as a know-it-all, as a brain on legs. It was certainly true that she'd always enjoyed philosophical discussions almost as much as the science and history lessons that were so dear to her heart.

But she had never once expected them to have a practical use.

'All right,' she said after a moment, and she grasped the Doctor's hand even more tightly. 'If it's the only way I'm going to get home…'

'That's the spirit,' said the Doctor brightly, starting to walk forward with Jude at his side. 'Just be positive. Think happy thoughts, good memories. Moments when you could have been selfish or hurtful but you chose not to.'

'All right,' said Jude. Her eyes were half-closed now, and she allowed herself to be guided forward by the Doctor. She glanced sideways at him – he was concerned, yes, that much was evident from his face. But he was absolutely determined, his strong jaw set forward. He was going to survive this, and save Jude's world, whatever the cost.

They took three more steps, right into the heart of the creature. It was like stepping outside and away from the warmth of a burning fire; the air was suddenly cold and still, and just for a moment there was silence.

Suddenly, someone, somewhere, was shouting out – overlapping cries of terror and anguish. It was only when the dark shadows flowed directly into Jude's mind that she understood – distantly, as if all this was happening to someone else – what the sounds were.

She and the Doctor were screaming.

Martha leapt away from the side of the boat as one of the lake creatures pushed its head through the splintered wood of the stern. The beast's stubby face reminded Martha of a shark, with ragged, random teeth and tiny eyes – three of them, arranged in a perfect triangle at the top of its head. The skull was ringed with forward-pointing horns, which ran like a frill around its neck. It resembled a bulldog that had grown a spiked collar out of its very flesh.

Saul was already on his feet – his legs wide and braced against the bucking of the boat – and he whirled the oar high over his head. He brought it down on the monster's head with a sharp *crack!*

The creature flinched and splashed back into the water. Though it retreated, other creatures were already moving into position, writhing over each other like alabaster worms.

Martha glanced around wildly. The water in the bottom of the boat was already ankle deep, and Petr was rowing for his life, struggling against the extra weight and the sudden fragility of the vessel. Saul stood, oars in his hands like paddle-ended spears, waiting for the next attack.

Assuming the boat wouldn't entirely fall apart in the meantime.

Jude was back at school, watching children swarming over the playing fields like ravaging ants. She was distant from them – distant and different. Shouted invitations to join in quickly became curses and jokes at her expense.

'Boring little bookworm! Boring little bookworm!'

Jude found herself turning away, not sure if this was a memory or a dream or something else altogether. She became aware of the wind tugging at her hair, a gentle breath on her cheeks that cooled her humiliation – and then a whispered voice, which she felt rather than heard.

Don't you want to hurt them? Make them suffer?

Jude turned, trying to isolate the source of the voice, trying to answer it in her own mind – but her thoughts seemed sluggish and uncontrollable, like logs caught in a slow, powerful river.

You could, you know. You're brighter than all of them – you could think of something.

'They're just little kids,' said Jude. Though she was aware of her lips moving, she wasn't sure if she was actually making a sound. 'They don't know any better.'

Like all your people, perhaps. So young, so… immature.

Now Jude thought about it, the voice sounded a little like the Doctor's – wise and thoughtful and cloaked in mystery. But it seemed to have no gender, no age, no accent. It was like every voice Jude had ever heard, rolled into one.

'We have lived here for centuries,' said Jude firmly, reacting more at the implied criticism of the entire village and its way of life than she had to the ridicule of the children.

You are young, and you have lived in peace for far too long. You have only recently encountered conflict and dissent…

Suddenly Jude was surrounded by fog, watching figures fighting in a small amphitheatre of light. Her eyes widened, she cried out – it was her father! And Uncle Petr was trying to throttle him!

She tried to run forward, but the fog held her in place, allowing the cold, empty voice to whisper once more into her ear.

This is what happens, you see. Free will, and then, within moments… betrayal and fighting and selfishness…

'No!' shouted Jude, though neither struggling figure seemed to hear her. 'They're good people. They must be… They must be confused.'

Would you not like to intercede? How far would you go to protect your father?

'I just want my father to be all right! But I like Petr as well. He's always been kind to me.'

The two fighting men vanished, the fog spinning Jude around and presenting one image after another: her mother forcing her to eat boiled yellow tubers ('They're good for you, make you big and strong!'), that lad at school she thought she'd liked but who ended up being a two-faced idiot ('I *pretended* to like you 'cos I wanted to get close to Leya – that's all'), the one argument she'd ever had with her father... She couldn't even remember what the circumstances were now, but Jude had ended up locked in her room without food for an entire day.

Don't you wish things were different?

The voice was quite insistent now, a harsh edge creeping in – Jude was reminded of a child, in danger of losing an argument, or a teacher whose authority was being questioned.

Memories and fears flashed around Jude in quick succession, a dizzying jumble of images and sounds. She forced her eyes shut and started to shout, to scream at the top of her voice, to force out confused words until her head throbbed with the effort of it all.

'I don't want to change *anything*,' she said. 'I did the best I can! Let me out of here!'

The boat pitched suddenly to one side. Martha felt her legs slide from beneath her. Saul pulled her to her feet just as a plume of spray and another sudden lurch announced the arrival of one of the shark-like creatures. This one seemed to want to hurl itself over the side of the boat. It landed awkwardly, making the entire craft list terrifyingly.

Even Saul was off balance now, and Martha slipped over and onto the floor. Within moments she was sliding towards the creature. Her trainers couldn't get a grip on the boat's soaked wooden boards. All she could see was the creature's gaping mouth.

Just in time, Martha was able to push herself to the side, avoiding the snapping jaws as the beast thrashed around. Her feet found purchase on the flattened edge of the boat; she twisted away from the great blunt head as it tried to find her.

There was a sudden ringing noise: Saul had unsheathed both swords. Though the boat was still at forty-five degrees to the lake's surface, he let out a battle shout and jumped nimbly towards the creature. First one blade, then the other, made silver arcs in the air. Martha instinctively glanced away.

The creature seemed barely to feel the attack. It arched its spine-covered tail high over its head, as if intending to smash it down against the matchstick boat.

Martha grabbed her chance, scrabbling for one of the oars that had come free and swinging it wildly towards the creature as it came at her.

Suddenly – and with a look that Martha would have sworn was a mixture of resentment and disappointment – the creature wriggled off the boat. With a huge, rending shrug of its entire body, it disappeared beneath the waves.

The boat rocked fiercely from side to side; Martha wondered for a moment if she were about to pitch over into the dark lake, but Saul's great arm steadied her. She was about to thank him when, with a roar of water and flesh, the wounded monster emerged once more, to the far side of the tiny ship. It brought its entire head down onto the boat, using its protective horns to smash through the wooden planks. Martha saw a crack appear beneath her feet; she wasn't sure how much punishment the little vessel could take.

Petr sprang to his feet, swinging at the attacking creature with one of the oars. Water was cascading into the boat now, over the side where the beast was pushing down, through numerous holes and splits in the tar-covered woodwork.

The monster snapped at Petr's oar, splintering it, then lunged towards them, hissing. Petr jumped out of the way just in time; within moments Saul was at his side, running forwards with swords outstretched.

The creature twisted sinuously, avoiding Saul's attack and raking its horns across the floor of the craft. In a flash its teeth snapped shut around Saul's legs.

Saul cried out, instinctively dropping both weapons and trying to escape, but the creature held firm. Martha jumped across to help, gripping Saul's arms while Petr held him about the torso. They were all waist deep in water now, only pockets of air trapped within the boat stopping it from sinking entirely. The one thing Martha cared about was releasing Saul from the jaws of the beast. But the man's legs were trapped, and he struggled desperately.

Suddenly, another creature lunged forward and out of the water – but its cavernous mouth was pointed towards its wounded fellow. It attacked, and withdrew, in the blink of an eye.

The creature attacking Saul immediately released its grip and, twitching uncontrollably, it slipped back into the lake.

The water around what was left of the boat was a frothing frenzy as the creatures piled one over another in their desperation to feed. Martha saw that the original beast, still flailing randomly, was now the focus of the attacks; leaching blood into the water, it was simply too tempting a target.

First one creature hurtled towards it through the water, snapping its jaws shut and then twisting around and around like a crocodile. A second soon followed. The suffering creature, now mortally wounded, attempted one brief retaliation. Countless more slid towards it, mouths gaping wide. Within moments the entire area was filled with white, overlapping shapes, the water frothing and foaming as if alive.

A low, injured cry – and the water now lapping at her chest – reminded Martha that her own predicament wasn't over yet. 'Come on,' said Petr, holding her arm and half-jumping, half-swimming back to where Saul had fallen.

The hunter had become caught on the large wooden board that normally housed the boat's main rower.

Behind him the entire prow of the craft was upright in the air, like the doomed *Titanic* recreated in miniature. Saul was silent and motionless but for the long, broken-sounding moans he made every few seconds.

Taking an arm each, and pushing through the splintered remains of the boat, Martha and Petr tugged Saul away from the water that broiled with the creatures. Saul's eyes suddenly shot open when his head and shoulders hit the cold water of the lake, and he began swimming as best he could, though Martha noticed that he wasn't using his legs. They trailed behind him like streamers of useless flesh and cloth.

The three swam furiously away from the boat as it slid entirely beneath the water, sometimes pausing to help each other, sometimes almost selfishly forcing tired arms and legs through the cold lake. Anything to put distance between them and the writhing predators. Martha hoped that the creatures would be more occupied with each other – and the huge, wounded beast that had prompted their feeding frenzy – than with the blood still seeping from Saul's legs.

Suddenly, out of the all-pervading blanket of fog, a dark shape began to form. Martha heard Petr almost whoop with joy. It seemed that these monsters patrolled only the deepest waters, and now Martha and the others were almost in reach of land – and safety.

Even Saul, who had been in danger of falling behind, seemed energised. Martha concentrated on her own progress, kicking for shore in desperation as much as relief. The water was colder than ever, and she couldn't stop shivering, swallowing mouthfuls of brackish water, but not caring if that meant she could emerge from the lake more quickly.

Still half-expecting to feel the vice-like grip of merciless jaws on her legs, still wondering if her aching arms and legs had any energy left in them, Martha forced herself up onto the rocky beach at the edge of the island. She collapsed for a moment, panting.

Petr was already standing and looking about him. 'I can't believe we're here,' he said quietly. 'All my life, we've looked out over the waters, but we never dared…' He looked down at Saul – only a villager could understand the importance of what they had just achieved. 'I never imagined I'd ever stand here.' He gripped his brother's hand, hauling him upright. 'Never dreamed *we'd* be the first to set foot on the island.'

And, just for a moment, a look of grim satisfaction passed between the brothers – a look of achievement and pride. A look of warmth and respect.

Martha, shivering, couldn't help but break the moment.

'Two questions,' she said. 'Do either of you really know what we're doing here?' She looked out over the dark waters of the lake, through the patchy fog, trying to see one last glimpse of the shark creatures. 'And how are we going to get back?'

FOURTEEN

Jude stumbled suddenly into blinding light, a cork popping out of darkness and dream. Her body was stiff, as if she had been asleep for a thousand years, and her mind fogged with images. Absolutely disorientated and blinded, she fell against an upright, dark shape – and cried out, thinking it was the creature again.

'It's OK,' said the Doctor, his voice calm and reassuring. 'It's me.'

'What happened?' asked Jude, still panicked and holding fast to the Doctor's arms.

'That creature was rummaging through our minds,' said the Doctor. 'For some reason, it decided that we should live.' And suddenly his face broke into a grin and he pointed at the dark shape further down the corridor. 'Doesn't look so frightening now we're this side of it, does it? Looks sort of… lonely.'

Jude turned, grinning. If they'd walked through the

creature, then that meant…

'That's right,' said the Doctor, turning his back on the dark angel. 'The heart of the *Castor*!' He jogged towards a huge door, rounded and formed of some bronze-hued metal, and almost embraced it, flinging his arms wide in every direction. 'Come on!' he called to a hesitant Jude. 'Nearly there!'

'Nearly there!' said Petr, pausing just for a moment. In truth, the island in the centre of the lake was at most only a few hundred square metres in size, but Saul had been unable to walk unaided and it had taken them some minutes to leave the beach. Now they approached the island's one feature – a great, rocky outcrop that rose up suddenly from the brown sand.

Martha risked a look back. Standing in the village, the island had not seemed very far away, but their journey had been daunting and now the cluster of buildings and houses was entirely invisible in the distant fog.

She turned back to Petr and Saul. Saul hadn't said much since their arrival on the island; he winced often when applying weight to his left leg, and Martha knew he was in a great deal of pain. She'd offered to check his wounds, but Saul had refused. However, he took advantage of this momentary lull to turn and glance at his older brother.

'Thank you,' he said simply, his voice sounding brittle and dry.

Petr glanced away. 'Those creatures would have killed us all. It was simply self-preservation.'

'I meant for not killing me back there!'

Petr stared at the dark, rocky outcrop, as if trying to read some meaning in its jagged edges and vertices. 'Would you have let me?' he said.

'I don't know.'

'Would you have deserved it?'

'Perhaps,' said Saul, after a moment's thought. 'Perhaps we all do.'

Petr nodded. 'That's true enough, I suppose.'

'I'm sorry for what happened,' said Saul. 'Between me and Kristine. I know just saying "sorry" isn't adequate, but—'

'You've destroyed my world!' said Petr suddenly. 'It's all over now. Everything's... *worthless*.' He looked around, a man conflicted between anger and tears. 'I don't know why we're here. Perhaps it's better that the village *is* destroyed!'

'You were preoccupied by your duties,' said Saul carefully. 'Kristine was lonely...'

Petr clapped his hands over his ears. 'I don't want to hear it!' he said. 'I don't want to listen to excuses!'

'There's no excuse for what happened,' said Saul simply.

'And the lies! And...' The next word came out as a whisper, a harsh prayer or a mournful curse. 'Thom...'

'You still love Thom,' said Saul, breathing heavily,

though with emotion or because of the pain, Martha wasn't quite sure.

Petr nodded slowly, rubbing a hand across his eyes. 'I do,' he said. 'I'm trying so hard to hate you – you, and Kristine, and Thom – but… I can't.' He looked around, glancing up at the starless sky and the distant shoreline, lost in the fog. 'Come on,' he said quietly.

Martha scrabbled around in the shingle, pulling out a long, water-smoothed piece of driftwood. She didn't know if the lake had tides, or if the wood was just some random detail of the entire bubble world's unreality, but it seemed sturdy enough, and she passed it over to Saul.

Saul grunted, forcing the stick under his arm like a crutch, before setting off for the rocky outcrop. The stunted spire of sharp stone at the heart of the island was bathed in diffuse light, great cracks and fissures becoming visible as the three travellers approached. Even more obvious was a great cave, concealed between an outreaching spur of rock on either side; it was like a dark mouth, slanted upwards, and Martha was reminded of the great maws of the creatures back in the lake.

They scrabbled over scree and jagged shingle as they neared the entrance, none of them sure what they were looking for, or knowing what to expect, but drawn by some simple, almost primal force towards the darkness. Martha supposed that, as a human, she had some innate urge to seek shelter in caves – and these people, however artificial their existence might be, were doubtless subject to the same drives. But she also felt a growing apprehension, for caves meant darkness and shadows and creeping, unseen things.

But a cave, at the centre of the island, seemingly in the centre of an artificial world… She suspected they'd find more there than just bat droppings and water dripping down stalactites.

Martha, suppressing a shiver and, with Petr and Saul close behind her, stepped into the echoing cavern.

The Doctor found some controls on the wall and within moments the door was rolling open.

Beyond was an enormous, rounded chamber, its walls punctuated with random red lights. By the time it had illuminated the floor and its occupant, the radiance took on a pinkish hue, giving the entire room an organic air.

Occupant.

Jude blinked quickly, not at all sure what she was looking at – but she understood, wordlessly, that she was looking at a person, not a *thing*.

The room was full of wires and tubes, but they were twisted and overlapping, creating complex patterns like a spider web covered in dew. In the centre, suspended some distance from the floor and slowly revolving and spinning, was some sort of creature. It had huge globular appendages that pulsed with an internal light but seemed more like additional brains or heads, and smaller limbs

– if that was the right word – that ebbed and flowed like hair in an invisible ocean. There was a central body, a bloated yet somehow still elegant succession of rounded shapes; most of the tubes and wires were attached here, the skin seeming pock-marked and blistered wherever the probes broke through the skin. Like the dark angel thing they had encountered, this entity seemed to fade and brighten from time to time. One moment it seemed almost invisible, as substantial as mist and memory; then it became full of force and flesh and was as real as anything that Jude had ever witnessed.

Jude could see no eyes or ears or mouth but, again, she knew somehow that this creature – this person – was quite capable of communication, despite the constraints of its surroundings.

The Doctor, too, was quiet and deferential. He walked further into the room only after a small sort-of bow, his hands slowly fidgeting behind his back. Jude somehow sensed that he was on unknown ground and was about to address an unfamiliar individual; he was, she suddenly decided, the best teacher she had ever encountered, if only because he himself was so keen to keep pushing back the barriers of his own knowledge and ignorance.

She wondered what his first words would be, how he would greet this emissary from faraway and perhaps unknowable worlds.

The Doctor paused, blinking for a moment, and then took another cautious step forward.

'I'm so sorry,' he said.

Of all the things Martha had expected to see in the cave, the last – barring, perhaps, an ice-cream van operated by her father and a crack squad of long-eared elves – was a door and the grinning form of the Dazai. The plain door was set into a cylinder of rock that ran from floor to ceiling in the middle of the chamber; the Dazai stood to one side, clearly both amused and delighted to see Martha and the others.

'What the hell are you doing here?' exclaimed Martha, as she stood in the centre of the cave, soaking wet, exhausted and still terrified beyond words.

'I went for a walk,' said the old woman simply. 'Long ago, I discovered that if you try to reach the far side of the lake, walk through a particular archway of trees... You end up here.'

Martha shook her head, puzzled and irritated in equal measure. She remembered her earlier return from the forest, and the strange topography of the land around the village; perhaps that explained why Petr and Saul seemed to unquestioningly accept what the old woman had just said.

'You've been here before, have you?'

The Dazai nodded, infuriatingly.

'And you didn't think to tell us about the shortcut? We've been attacked, half-eaten, shipwrecked...'

'Petr and Saul needed some time together,' said the

Dazai. 'There were some… matters that needed their undivided attention.'

'Wasn't there a safer way of doing things?' asked Martha.

'Perhaps,' said the Dazai. 'But it worked, didn't it?'

And she glanced over at the brothers, who were supporting each other, arms wrapped around each other's shoulders.

'What's going on?' said Martha, dimly aware of the note of hysteria creeping into her voice. 'What's this door in aid of? Who *are* you?' She felt on the verge of tears, though she wasn't quite sure why – perhaps it was just having had the rug pulled out from under her feet once too often.

'I'm just someone who follows her instincts,' said the Dazai. 'All other forms of knowledge… have their limits.'

'Oh, very Zen!' said Martha.

The Dazai smiled, the sort of relaxed smile that just made Martha want to go and do something very un-Zen-like. 'Something told me it was important for the brothers to at least begin the process of reconciliation,' said the Dazai. 'The land and the people are one, after all.'

Martha remembered the Doctor having said something similar recently. In fact, now that she thought about it, he was the only other person she'd ever met who could be infuriating and wonderful and frustrating, all in the same breath.

'This is the heart of our world,' continued the old woman. 'I come here often to think. Of course, I wasn't about to tell anyone else that. The island, the far side of the shore – they're all off limits, and rightly so.' And she nodded and bowed towards Petr, with a glance both recognising and overthrowing his petty laws and regulations.

'And this door?' Now that Martha looked at it, there was the faintest impression of the space station decor, resembling the shadow of the portal she and the Doctor had seen in the forest. But this was definitely a real, solid, physical door, seemingly carved out of the same stone as the surrounding pillar.

'It has never opened for me,' said the Dazai. 'I am a part of this world, and am constrained by it. You, on the other hand…' And she gestured to the great stone door with her pale, bony hand.

Martha stepped forward uncertainly. She was suddenly reminded of the Disney King Arthur film she'd seen as a kid, and was grateful that there wasn't any sword to pull out of this particular stone, or some other expected show of strength. In fact, she couldn't see anything remotely resembling a handle, or hinges, or a doorknob. It was simply one great slab of stone set inside a similar vertical block.

She paused, aware of everyone's eyes on her, and let her hand rest on the rock. The pillar pulsed imperceptibly; it was as if she was resting her palm on the outer covering of some vast and distant machine.

Moments later there was a click. The entire door, now a centimetre proud of the surrounding stone, was edged with a pinkish brightness. Martha took a step backwards, and the door swung open further. Beyond it Martha could see only pulsing red light. Given that the rocky structure was about the same width as the TARDIS, Martha wasn't sure if this was some sort of teleport, or if it led to impossible rooms – or if it was simply a brightly lit, hollowed-out space.

'Go on,' said the Dazai, her voice calm and soothing.

Martha stepped into the light, and immediately everything around her changed. She found herself in a rounded room, criss-crossed with a web of wires and tubes, dominated by an impossible, floating creature. To one side stood the Doctor; to the other, Saul's daughter, diminutive, but brave, despite her surroundings.

'Doctor!' she cried out in unabashed delight, ignoring her surroundings, ignoring everything, and running towards him. She threw her arms around him, laughing.

The Doctor smiled, feigning a casual indifference. 'I was wondering if you were going to turn up!'

'Why?'

The Doctor did not respond. Instead, a voice, a whisper, pushed its way into Martha's mind; as clear as a struck bell, as quiet as a recalled memory.

Now we are all together.

Martha saw Jude turn away from the pulsing creature at the centre of the room. 'That voice,' she said to the Doctor. 'It sounds like the angel.'

'It's similar, yes,' said the Doctor.

'Angel?' queried Martha.

'There's a creature on this station,' explained the Doctor. 'A dark angel, you could say – the sum of human evil.'

'The moving signal on the scanner…'

The Doctor nodded. 'Imbued with the life of two universes, the ship could – near enough – keep track of the creature. Just as it appears to hover between our reality and another, so the *Castor*'s instruments can pick up its intermittent signals.'

'It's attacked the Doctor twice,' said Jude simply. 'And me once,' she added. She shivered. 'It was horrible.'

'We should have died, been torn apart by our own desires and fears and capacity for evil,' continued the Doctor.

'What happened?' Martha asked.

The Doctor turned to the creature hanging in the centre of the room. Martha noticed that even he was unsure which appendage or protuberance he should be addressing; he made do with a little nod of courtesy. 'I was hoping you could answer that,' he said.

The creature shifted slightly, changing the angle of its eternal rotation.

Your friend decided to stay in the unreal world. I have rarely seen such bravery.

The Doctor winked at Martha. 'I'm not surprised,' he said, turning back to the creature. 'You have only seen the very worst side of human nature. As I said before… I'm truly sorry.'

'What's going on?' whispered Martha.

The Doctor turned on the spot, indicating the entire chamber with his outstretched arms. 'This is the heart of the *Castor* – and this is its ultimate prisoner. Its ultimate experiment.' He spat the last word with distaste.

I was a traveller through the dimensions. Creatures captured me, tortured me, kept me here.

'Why?' asked Martha.

The Doctor replied. 'Our friend has many unique properties. One of them is the ability to soak up emotions and memories and instincts. If you're a traveller or a researcher it beats taking notes, I suppose. Anyway, some human scientists captured him. They decided, if they attached the right technology, they could take people of unthinkable evil… and *tame* them. They wanted to hook them up, suck out the evil, and make them good again!'

'But the Doctor believes good and evil are choices we make, not… flaws in our minds,' said Jude quietly.

The Doctor nodded energetically, like a teacher commending a pupil. 'Even if it had worked,' he said, 'you're only making as many problems as you're trying to solve. You strip away some memories, fair enough – but unless you replace the human mind with a robot brain, you've still got the problem of free will. As Jude says, life is all about the decisions we make – to flee from evil, or to confront it. To jump through a door, or to stay behind because someone needs you.' And he smiled at Martha once more.

And I could not stand the evil that flowed into me…

The Doctor rested a hand on the insubstantial creature. It solidified, then seemed to disappear, then blinked back into existence again. 'Our friend is more than a mere sponge,' said the Doctor. 'Imagine what it was forced to endure, to witness – to experience even. Every killing, every crime, every evil desire, lived and relived, over and over again.'

I had to get rid of the evil. I had to find a way to… stay sane.

Martha nodded. 'And so this angel creature…'

As if on cue, a dark, shrouded shape flowed through the solid wall and pooled in a corner. It was tall and wraith-like; Martha reckoned the 'dark angel' description was as good as any.

'An attempt to expel all the evil,' said the Doctor. 'But eventually it took on a life of its own – an evil life, of course. The prisoners and staff who didn't turn on each other were… butchered… by this "dark angel". Butchered from within.'

The creature in the heart of the chamber shifted

again, changing colour slightly as if indicating its state of mind.

I can't always control it. I did not want to kill, but... There was nothing I could do.

There was a pause, Martha finding herself transfixed by the awful shadow in the corner of the room. Was it her imagination, or was it becoming darker, and seemingly taking on a more solid form? Moment by moment, was it inching closer to them?

I needed another outlet. Another... arena, in which I could explore my feelings. What I had experienced, what I had seen...

'The village!' exclaimed Martha.

The Doctor smiled. 'A free space in which humanity could be explored, analysed and observed.'

'So it's like playing *The Sims* – but with real people.'

'Exactly – thought made flesh! The bubble world is partly powered by an entirely different dimension, maintained and guided by the *Castor*'s last prisoner.' The Doctor again turned to the floating mass in the centre of the room, smiling as if greeting a long-lost friend. 'In our universe, you have so many powers – so much insight, so much to offer... And they kept you trapped in the dark, a creature to be experimented on. A creature to be *used*.'

The one thing I could not do was escape. I am now a part of this place, and it is part of me. I could only experience life through the world I had created...

'But isn't that amazing?' exclaimed the Doctor, wheeling around like a theatrical showman. 'Over the years... Life gave birth to life, life evolved and changed... Life became real and sentient, capable of great emotion – capable of true choice. Capable of good and evil!'

It was once an innocent world, a world with parameters. They are breaking down...

'That's a *good* thing,' said the Doctor, draping an arm around Jude. 'Take my friend Jude here. She's thinking for herself, she's making her own choices... She can even leave her world and exist within this ship!' He puffed out his cheeks, a picture of simple delight. 'You know, life never ceases to amaze me!'

'That's all very well,' said Martha, 'but in Jude's world, the children are disappearing.'

Energy, said the creature simply. *It is all slipping away from me...*

'The *Castor* has been in this dark area of space for too long,' said the Doctor. 'It's running out of power. Even a strict regime of day and night hasn't solved the problem. So the children have disappeared, the geography of the world has been truncated and looped...'

'Why the children?' asked Martha. 'You said earlier that it was just random. So why not adults or babies – or even the monsters in the forest?'

The Doctor threw his arms around Jude again. 'When you're a kid, your mind is *bursting* with fears and dreams and daft ideas! You can believe six impossible things before breakfast, and still have room for a multitude more!'

'Children require more energy than adults,' observed Martha.

'You ask any parent,' agreed the Doctor. 'And with our friend here running out of processing power... Desperate times call for desperate measures.'

'So the children simply disappeared...'

The Doctor nodded. 'Like files deleted from a hard drive.'

'But why did we see them?' said Jude. 'The figures in the fog...'

The creature stirred again, what appeared to be veins just under its skin taking on a purple hue.

I wanted to show... compassion. I had to offer hope.

'But at the same time,' the Doctor went on, 'the creator of Jude's world knew it was a dangerous strategy. It could run out of energy – it could die – at almost any minute.'

'Taking the bubble world with it,' said Martha. 'No wonder the prophecies were so gloomy.'

I need energy from this universe as well as my own. I have persisted and struggled... but to no avail.

'You've got to keep trying!' said the Doctor.

Perhaps it is time for all this to end. To maintain the world, to protect you from the evil thoughts I expelled...

Martha glanced over at the shadow creature. It was only a few metres away now, and seemingly bigger than ever.

I'm so tired. Perhaps I should just let it all end.

'No!' said the Doctor urgently. 'Hundreds of lives rely on you. You can't just give in.'

It was an interesting experiment. I have seen some good, some love, some positive choices being made… But I do not think them sufficient to balance the evil I have experienced.

'You can't mean that,' said the Doctor. Martha noticed that Jude was clinging to him now, her precociousness overtaken by simple, understandable fear. 'You can't allow an entire culture to die!'

The dark shadow creature, and the vast prisoner suspended in the centre of the room, began to pulse as one.

Do not worry, came the same calm, measured voice in Martha's mind. *It will be painless.*

FIFTEEN

Martha couldn't move. At first she thought the creature suspended in the centre of the room had, like some legendary Gorgon, turned her to stone. Then she wondered if it wasn't simply shock – shock prompted by the uncomplicated way the quiet voice had announced the death of an entire world.

Slowly, however, she became aware of someone standing behind her. 'Don't worry,' came the voice. 'Everything will be all right.'

The voice was human – and full of quiet confidence and subtle determination.

With great effort Martha was able to twist her head; behind her stood the Dazai. For the second time that day, the old woman's simple, uncomplicated presence was a source of both relief and consternation.

'How long have you been there?' Martha asked.

'Long enough to understand what's going on. Long

enough to know…' The Dazai looked around the room with its pooled red lights and criss-crossed wires with something like awe clear on her face. 'I'm not sure I believe in God, but one thing I understand – as far as my people are concerned, I am in the presence of our Creator.'

Behind the Dazai was a column of light, approximately the size and shape of the pillar of rock in the cave. When the old woman entirely stepped through, it faded from sight.

So tired, came the voice in Martha's mind. *I want to end it all.*

'Nonsense!' said the Dazai, striding forward with surprising speed. 'How can a creature as wonderful as you ever be tired of life?'

The Doctor seemed energised by the Dazai's hopefulness; with arms almost flapping in delight, and entirely ignoring the black shadow that was nearly within touching distance, he hopped from foot to foot in front of the creature. 'She's right, you know! You've seen some terrible things, and it's little wonder that you wonder about the value of life itself, but… surely the glimmers of triumphant free will, the acts of bravery and courage…'

They are not enough. Things are still skewed to darkness.

'I refuse to believe that,' said the Dazai firmly. 'I have lived for many, many years. Some say I am as old as the village. I know for sure that I have seen many strange and contradictory things. But I also know that light conquers darkness – given time.'

A tired saying. Your words are hollow and empty. I do not believe them.

The Doctor paused. 'A long time ago, on Earth, a young man was arrested and sentenced to death for treason by the Tsar. Dressed in a white gown and blindfolded, he was led to the square for a public execution. Bound to a post, the firing squad prepared to fire. "Ready – aim…" Rifles were cocked, fingers rested on triggers – and only at the last possible moment did a rider come with a message of reprieve.'

What is your point?

'The young man felt he had a second chance at life. He became one of the greatest writers the planet ever produced. His novels are dark, they grapple with evil – but they are also full of unwarranted mercy. In one a character says, "I do not know the answer to the problem of evil – but I do know love."'

Love?

'These people deserve to be shown love and compassion. They are relying on your mercy,' continued the Doctor.

'Please,' said Jude, sobbing. 'I don't want to die!'

But I am tired. So tired…

'I can pilot this ship to a brighter part of the universe,' said the Doctor. 'Well away from prying eyes, but close enough to stars for the *Castor* to recharge itself.'

But I can't keep the darkness quiet any longer. The things I have seen...

There was an agonised tone in the creature's voice; Martha noticed that the shadowy angel was now as tall and as wide as the room itself and it was almost within touching distance of the Doctor and Jude.

'Ah,' said the Dazai, weighing up the angel slowly. 'I wonder if I may be able to help with that...'

And with that she stepped forward, bravely and quite deliberately. With a final smile, and her frail arms outstretched, she walked straight into the shadow.

She flowed into the angel, and the angel flowed into her; an impossible figure and a prosaic one merging and overlapping like the meeting of wind and fog. The Dazai cried out in unendurable agony, her tiny body writhing and twisting in black shrouds and shadow.

Freed from the strange paralysis that had overcome her, Martha ran immediately to her – but the Doctor smoothly interposed himself. 'It's OK,' he said. 'Just leave her for a minute.'

'But it'll kill her!'

'I'm not so sure,' said the Doctor. 'Look!'

The Dazai had fallen onto her back now, staring up at the vaulted ceiling with sightless eyes. Her arms and legs were shaking, her thin lips pulled tight in wordless agony – Martha couldn't even begin to imagine the tormented images rushing through her mind.

Then, brushing aside the Doctor's offered arm, the

Dazai got to her feet. The shadow creature seemed to have entirely vanished – or been absorbed within her tiny frame. Though unsteady, and still shaking from her experiences, there was a strange, detached look on the Dazai's face – she seemed almost younger, the worst of her wrinkles smoothed away, her eyes burning brightly. But there was obvious pain in her eyes, a sorrow so deep and so acute that Martha had to glance away.

It was like looking into the Doctor's eyes when he alluded to his home and his people.

'Oh…' The Dazai shook her head slowly, as if in disbelief. 'Oh,' she whispered again, a long, drawn-out sigh as silent tears began to course down her cheeks.

The effect on the creature in the centre of the room – and the voice that Martha and the others heard – was even more remarkable.

It's all… gone. I am free of it all!

'That's right,' said the Doctor, a soothing note in his voice. 'You can just concentrate on sustaining your world – on enjoying everything that you have created!'

I no longer feel… guilt. It is not my fault any more!

'It never was,' said the Doctor quietly. He placed a reassuring arm around Jude. 'Just you concentrate on keeping the bubble world ticking over. At least until you get to a new star system. People like my friend Jude here are depending on you!'

I think I may be able to manage more than that.

Suddenly the room flickered, the wires and artificial

lighting replaced with the rough stone cave on the island. The two regions became one, just as they had when Martha and the Doctor had first attempted to return to the *Castor* from the forest.

Petr and Saul stood to one side of the great stone column, eyes and mouths wide, understanding nothing. 'Doctor?' said Petr, a note of panic in his voice. 'Where are we?'

The suspended creature pulsed brightly.

With less to think about, less to control… I should be able to…

Once more the stone column split open, a door sliding back to reveal a square of impossible brightness. Small, dark figures moved impatiently in the light, stepping one by one out onto the floor of the chamber.

The missing children.

Within moments, the cave was full of the sounds of laughter and quick feet and boundless delight. Petr, dropping his swords to the floor, threw himself across the room, wrapping one boy in his arms and weeping uncontrollably.

'Thom! Thom!' Petr was sobbing, absolutely unashamed and innocent, like a baby.

The boy returned the embrace. 'Dad!' He hugged Petr tight, as if desperate for these physical sensations after a period of dreaming limbo. 'What happened to us?'

'I don't know,' said Petr. 'What matters is that you are back!'

Martha prodded Jude gently, for the girl was still looking around, baffled by the two overlapping realities and the sudden appearance of the lost children. 'I think your dad wants to see you,' said Martha with a grin.

Jude ran across the room, her arms wide, as if finally acknowledging that making sense of it all would have to wait. She hurled herself into Saul's embrace; he winced and stumbled slightly, but said nothing, lost in the joy of reunion.

Martha smiled. She could sense the creature's delight – freed of the shackles of other people's evil, and revelling in the confused babble of voices and stories, the final prisoner of the research station *Castor* was doing what the Doctor had ordered – enjoying the world that it had created.

'You gave me such a fright!' Saul was saying, still clinging tightly to his daughter. 'Promise me you'll never wander off like that again!'

'Don't make me promise something you know I can't keep!' Jude was giggling, just a normal child teasing her father. 'But, if it makes you feel better... I'll not go wandering – for the next couple of weeks, anyway!'

Petr stood tall, his face smudged with tears and dirt. 'Listen to me, everyone!' he said loudly. The children stopped jumping and shouting, looking instead towards their leader in hushed deference. 'We should return to the village – there are lots of people who want to see you again!'

'And how are you going to cross the lake?' asked Martha, ever the pragmatist.

'The Dazai has her methods,' said Petr, 'and so do I.'

It was only then, as the children began to file out of the cave, that Martha caught the creature's voice in her own mind.

Trust me, Petr. Lead your people back to the village!

Martha ran to the cave's entrance and looked out. The sky was full of stars now, not an empty void; light fell down on a lake that was perfectly calm, and a village liberated from fog. As if in recognition of all that had happened, the lanterns that had filled the village hall were now spreading across the bridges and pathways and lanes, bathing houses and workplaces with light and warmth.

Between the island and the shore near the village there now stretched a spur of rock. Water still flowed down its sides, as if it had only this moment emerged from the lake like a long, sinuous creature coming up for air.

For all Martha knew, that's exactly what the creature had called into existence. This world belonged to the alien creature; it could, she supposed, do exactly what it liked with it.

Martha stood for a moment, watching the excited children scamper across the land bridge. They were already swapping stories of heroes and dark angels. She hoped the causeway would remain a permanent feature of Jude's world – she could imagine generations of people coming here and creating their own legends about today's events.

And, perhaps, Jude would tell her own children of a traveller from beyond the stars, of seeing the 'real world' that existed beyond and behind the trees and houses and lake, of battling dark angels and pleading for her life before a creature with godlike powers. And her kids wouldn't believe a word of it, and rightly so. It would become a tall tale, alluded to and mocked, and, over the centuries, a myth, fit only for arguments and dreams.

Petr and Saul passed by, about to start their journey over the causeway. Jude and Thom played in front of them, just kids happy to be alive – and glad to be going home. Saul was walking unaided now, but Martha could sense that the silent distance between the brothers was less than it had been. Their eyes, as both men made a nodding motion towards her, seemed to say as much: problems would be faced, not ignored. It might not be easy or pleasant, but compared to what they had both faced together, it would be the simplest thing in the world.

She also saw in their eyes a queried goodbye, an invitation to follow them both back to the village, or to drift away as she saw fit.

Martha grinned – if she knew the Doctor, it would be the latter.

She glanced back into the cave. The Doctor and the Dazai were on their own now, talking quietly by the stone pillar that was, once more, a plain and featureless outcrop of rock. To their side, the suspended creature pulsed gently, its own environment of straight lines and tubes fading in and out of sight.

Martha came over to stand at the Doctor's side. 'What will you do now?' the Doctor was asking quietly.

'The things I have seen…' The Dazai's voice was even more brittle than usual, as if the poor woman had been forced to run a marathon. 'The emotions that are flowing through me…' Martha noticed that the Dazai's hands were claws, permanently tensed like sharpened bones covered with paper-thin flesh. 'I *think* I can control them, make sense of it all… But I must leave the village. I must retreat into the forests and the mountains. There I can harm no one, influence no one – I can simply battle with my demons.'

'You're incredibly brave,' said Martha suddenly.

The Dazai shrugged. 'Perhaps I'm just doing what is expected of me. Legend has it that each Dazai must retreat from the village, and battle with their own monsters, before they can be considered truly worthy of the title.'

'You'll return,' said the Doctor, though there was a trace of uncertainty in his voice. 'Eventually.'

'Perhaps,' the Dazai responded. 'Perhaps, one day, I will go back. But for the moment…' And she looked out, not at the clustered buildings, but at the surrounding mountains and forests. The sun was just starting to rise, illuminating treetops and the flags and banners of the village.

'Good luck,' said the Doctor.

The Dazai twisted her face into a smile. 'I don't need *luck*,' she said, a little of her old belligerence returning, and then she moved away.

Martha glanced at the creature, still suspended in its awful cocoon of technology, but seemingly quiet and content now. She hoped that, free of other people's evil, it would find some sort of peace while watching over its created world.

When she looked back, the Dazai had gone, taking the last traces of the dark angel with her. The cave, with its view of the land bridge and the blue-green lake and its central pillar of rock, came into focus one last time – and then disappeared from view.

Martha and the Doctor were back with the extra-dimensional creature on the *Castor*, and the TARDIS could only be a few corridors away.

The Doctor walked over to the prisoner, the god of the unreal world, and patted its flank. 'Thank you,' he said simply. And then, after a pause, 'You really are amazing!'

He turned to Martha.

'You're not so bad yourself, you know. If you hadn't gone back and tried to rescue Saul…'

His eyes were distant, as if he – uniquely – could see through the walls of the *Castor*. Perhaps, just for a moment, he saw a dark forest and an island at the heart of a mysterious lake – and a village of flags and bridges, celebrating the return of its children.

'How did you rescue Saul from the monster?' he asked suddenly.

'Ah,' said Martha modestly. 'I did have a little help.'

'Well, you can tell me later,' said the Doctor. 'I love a good story – heroes and monsters, that sort of thing.' He turned back to the creature. 'Like I said – give me a minute and we'll get you somewhere warm,' he said. 'And then you can drift again, far away from humans and all the evil things they do.' He glanced at Martha. 'Present company excepted, of course.'

'Then back to the TARDIS?' said Martha.

The Doctor nodded. 'Yes. Back to the TARDIS.' He turned to the doorway. 'I can access the *Castor*'s navigation systems from just down here…'

Martha followed him out of the angular chamber. Their feet rang out on the metal walkway as they strolled away.

'I don't quite understand why the ship's scanners didn't pick up that creature,' said Martha as they walked. 'It made a stab at tracking that shadow thing.'

'Well,' said the Doctor, 'that big *splurge* of data… Maybe it wasn't just the bubble world it was detecting – but the creature as well. It's a very fine line, between creator and creation.'

'And what will happen if the *Castor* drifts into darkness again?' queried Martha.

The Doctor smiled. 'Let's hope I do as good a job next time,' said the Doctor. 'Let's hope I have someone with me as... brave as you were.'

'What do you mean, "next time"?'

'Oh, just something the Dazai said. She sort of implied that this had happened before. That the biggest lessons in life we need to learn again and again.'

'And what lesson do we learn from all this? Not to go exploring when you find yourself in a forest in deep space?'

'Oh, yeah, *that*,' said the Doctor with a grin. 'And...' He risked a final glance over his shoulder. 'To be capable of love, nine times out of ten... Someone needs to love us first.'

Acknowledgements

Thanks to Russell T Davies and Justin Richards, for allowing me to write this footnote to the glory that is New *Who*, to my wife and family – Helen, Emily and Charlotte – for time, space and macadamia nuts, and to Terry Barker, Mike Chappell, Paul Cornell, Simon Forward, Nev Fountain, Matthew Graham, Dominic Lord at Jill Foster Ltd, Moray Laing, Mike Maddox, Steven Moffat, John McLaughlin and Charlotte Bruton at Campbell Thomson & McLaughlin, Helen Raynor, Gareth Roberts, Gary Russell, Rob Shearman, James Sinden, Keith Topping, Steve Tribe, and all the Unusual Suspects, for lots of other things.

DOCTOR · WHO

THE CLOCKWISE MAN
by Justin Richards

THE MONSTERS INSIDE
by Stephen Cole

WINNER TAKES ALL
by Jacqueline Rayner

THE DEVIANT STRAIN
by Justin Richards

ONLY HUMAN
by Gareth Roberts

THE STEALERS OF DREAMS
by Steve Lyons

Also available from BBC Books
featuring the Doctor and Rose
as played by David Tennant and Billie Piper:

DOCTOR·WHO

THE STONE ROSE
by Jacqueline Rayner

THE FEAST OF THE DROWNED
by Stephen Cole

THE RESURRECTION CASKET
by Justin Richards

THE NIGHTMARE OF BLACK ISLAND
by Mike Tucker

THE ART OF DESTRUCTION
by Stephen Cole

THE PRICE OF PARADISE
by Colin Brake

Also available from BBC Books
featuring the Doctor and Martha
as played by David Tennant and Freema Agyeman:

DOCTOR·WHO

Sting of the Zygons
by Stephen Cole

ISBN 978 1 84607 225 3

UK £6.99 US $11.99/$14.99 CDN

The TARDIS lands the Doctor and Martha in the
Lake District in 1909, where a small village has been
terrorised by a giant, scaly monster. The search is on
for the elusive 'Beast of Westmorland', and explorers,
naturalists and hunters from across the country are
descending on the fells. King Edward VII himself is
on his way to join the search, with a knighthood for
whoever finds the Beast.

But there is a more sinister presence at work in the Lakes
than a mere monster on the rampage, and the Doctor
is soon embroiled in the plans of an old and terrifying
enemy. As the hunters become the hunted, a desperate
battle of wits begins – with the future of the entire world
at stake…

DOCTOR·WHO

The Last Dodo

by Jacqueline Rayner

ISBN 978 1 84607 224 6

UK £6.99 US $11.99/$14.99 CDN

The Doctor and Martha go in search of a real live dodo, and are transported by the TARDIS to the mysterious Museum of the Last Ones. There, in the Earth section, they discover every extinct creature up to the present day, all still alive and in suspended animation.

Preservation is the museum's only job – collecting the last of every endangered species from all over the universe. But exhibits are going missing…

Can the Doctor solve the mystery before the museum's curator adds the last of the Time Lords to her collection?

Creatures and Demons

by Justin Richards

ISBN 978 1 84607 229 1

UK £7.99 US $12.99/$15.99 CDN

Throughout his many adventures in time and space, the Doctor has encountered aliens, monsters, creatures and demons from right across the universe. In this third volume of alien monstrosities and dastardly villains, *Doctor Who* expert and acclaimed author Justin Richards describes some of the evils the Doctor has fought in over forty years of time travel.

From the grotesque Abzorbaloff to the monstrous Empress of the Racnoss, from giant maggots to the Daleks of the secret Cult of Skaro, from the Destroyer of Worlds to the ancient Beast itself… This book brings together more of the terrifying enemies the Doctor has battled against.

Illustrated throughout with stunning photographs and design drawings from the current series of *Doctor Who* and his previous 'classic' incarnations, this book is a treat for friends of the Doctor whatever their age, and whatever planet they come from…

DOCTOR·WHO

The Inside Story

by Gary Russell

ISBN 978 0 56348 649 7

£14.99

In March 2005, a 900-year-old alien in a police public call box made a triumphant return to our television screens. *The Inside Story* takes us behind the scenes to find out how the series was commissioned, made and brought into the twenty-first century. Gary Russell has talked extensively to everyone involved in the show, from the Tenth Doctor himself, David Tennant, and executive producer Russell T Davies, to the people normally hidden inside monster suits or behind cameras. Everyone has an interesting story to tell.

The result is the definitive account of how the new *Doctor Who* was created. With exclusive access to design drawings, backstage photographs, costume designs and other previously unpublished pictures, *The Inside Story* covers the making of all twenty-six episodes of Series One and Two, plus the Christmas specials, as well as an exclusive look ahead to the third series.